Shankar Vedantam has excelled in succ .... the
people of Jammu and Kashmir. Both fiction and non-fiction pieces are free
flowing and very readable. This book is a must read, and ought to be added
to every library and personal collection.

Admiral L Ramdas
Winner of the Magsaysay Award for Peace and International Understanding;
President Emeritus, Pakistan-India Peoples' Forum for Peace and Democracy

***

Shankar Vedantam is one of the finest writers we have published in recent
years. His clear and incisive prose in The Scoop brought an all too believable
reporter to life, while simultaneously illustrating the ironies and complexities
of life in modern India.

J. Rod Clark
Editor, Rosebud Magazine

***

The most striking aspect of Vedantam's writing is his journalistic reportage
style of rendition. This dramatic style makes his characters - Madan Doha
Singh, in particular - an observer-reporter of events in which he himself is
an active participant. "I am the place in which something has occurred,"
said the French anthropologist Claude Levi-Strauss.
In The Ghosts of Kashmir, the self becomes a site of turmoil, mirroring
the political turmoil of the landscape. The stories in this collection explore
different genres and offer the reader an engaging and thought-provoking
experience.

Shona Ramaya
Editor, *Catamaran*, a magazine of South Asian American writing

The Ghosts of Kashmir

Shankar Vedantam

Biography

Shankar Vedantam is a national staff writer at *The Washington Post*. Besides journalism, Vedantam also writes fiction and plays. His short stories have been published in *Rosebud* and *Catamaran* magazines. *Tom, Dick & Harriet*, a play he co-authored with Donald C. Drake, was produced in Philadelphia at the Brick Playhouse in April 2004. Vedantam's second play, *Flying While Brown*, was about civil liberties in America after the 9/11 attacks. The winner of numerous awards and fellowships, Vedantam is also the author of *When Violence Masquerades as Virtue: A Brief History of Terrorism*, part of the 2003 book *Violence or Dialogue*, published by the International Psychoanalytic Association. *The Ghosts of Kashmir* is Vedantam's first collection of short stories.

Can you, every one of you,
lay your hand on your heart and say that every sufferer,
whether Hindu, Sikh or Muslim,
is your own brother or sister? This is the test for you.

Mohandas K. Gandhi,
Prayer Meeting, November 12, 1947

I see the world is mad.
If I tell the truth, they rush to beat me.
If I lie, they trust me.

Saint Kabir
15th century Indian poet

Acknowledgements

My debts are large. Many people helped shape this book. Most – teachers, friends, colleagues – will go unmentioned, but they are not unremembered.

First, Ma and Dad, for showing me the joy of words and language. Gayatri and Vish, for being both anchor and beacon.

Baba and Abhi, for being free spirits.

Anuj Bahri Malhotra and Laurie Liss, for believing.

J. Rod Clark and Shona Ramaya, who helped me believe.

Simone Zelitch and all my friends at Café 90, who helped me start.

Manil Suri and Aparna Devare, who helped me finish and Ashwini Tambe, quite simply, for everything.

— *Shankar Vedantam*

The Ghosts of Kashmir

Shankar Vedantam

tara press, new delhi

India Research Press
B-4/22, Safdarjung Enclave, New Delhi – 110 029.
Ph.: 24694610; Fax : 24618637
www.indiaresearchpress.com
contact@indiaresearchpress.com ; bahrisons@vsnl.com

2005
Shankar Vedantam ©® 2005 India Research Press

ISBN : 81-87943-79-3

Cataloging in Publication Data
Shankar Vedantam
THE GHOSTS OF KASHMIR
by Shankar Vedantam

Collection of Short Stories.
1. Kashmir   2. Fiction - Indian   3. Kashmiri people.
4. Threat   5. Turmoil   6. Liberation
        I. Title.   II. Author

Printed in India at Focus Impressions, New Delhi – 110 003.

for my parents,
who made it possible
and for Ashwini,
who made it necessary

Contents

The Fanatic   1

The Scoop   41

Rain   55

Sakina   81

The Gentleman's Game   121

Major Mishra's Secret   131

The Ghosts of Kashmir   149

Fear In The Valley   173

The Fanatic

In the early days of his marriage, Ismail often emerged from his morning shower to find Nasreen outside the bathroom. She would take him by the hand, pull him down to the fluffy rug beside their bed, and make love to him. When he argued it would make him late for work, it only increased her desire and, at least in the beginning, desire got the better of him, too.

Delay was not the only reason Ismail disapproved of the morning encounters: He did not know what to make of Nasreen's casual command of the sexual initiative. Why, he asked himself, did they have to have sex on the floor when the bed was only a step away? And why did they have to keep changing positions when one was good enough? He had a vague sense that Nasreen's lack of inhibition was somehow connected to the scores of books she devoured and her interest in foreign movies. Abid was conceived during one of these morning encounters. The pregnancy made short work of the practice and, after their son was born, Nasreen began to lay Ismail's pressed clothes on the bed, place a fresh muslin cloth beside them, and pull the bedroom door shut behind her. When Ismail now emerged from his shower, he heard Nasreen bustling about the house or playing with Abid. He would stand on the fluffy rug as he dressed, feeling the ticklish fibres with a mixture of relief and regret.

At the start of the month, when customers at his sweet shop were flush with payday cash, Ismail worked as late as eleven o'clock. By the end of the month, or during lean times, he finished at nine. Abid, who grew into a model child, was often in bed by the time the shopkeeper got home. Ismail left all decisions about the household to Nasreen. She scheduled birthday parties, decided when the house needed repainting and planned their Sunday evening outings. He knew her competence far exceeded any challenge that running the house could offer. He was vaguely grateful that she seemed satisfied. She had never sought a job, although she could have easily found one. He wondered about this, but never aloud, out of fear that it might prompt her in a direction he did not intend.

As the years passed, Nasreen developed a group of friends whom she invited to the house to discuss politics and culture. She called these meetings "soirees," a word Ismail never pronounced correctly. They started at seven o'clock and often were still in progress when Ismail got home from work. He never participated in these gatherings – the topics held no interest for him. But he never begrudged Nasreen the company of people who were unlike himself. Most of Nasreen's friends knew Ismail only slightly. Some did not know him at all. At the same time, as Abid finished school and entered college, barely a handful of Ismail's customers learned that he was married. There were some people who were both her friends and his customers, but they didn't connect the vastly different worlds to the same household.

Ismail's shop eventually became a thriving establishment in Bangalore. Each evening, crowds gathered before the brightly lit glass display. Like moths, the customers stabbed at the glass with their fingers and yelled requests until Ismail filled their cardboard boxes with sweets. Most appended "brother" to his name. Elderly women called him "son." Generations of children came to associate his name with rewards for finished homework, bribes for doing household chores and the celebration of birthdays. Street children hung around his shop at closing time. As the rush of customers thinned out, they fought each other for brooms to sweep the shop and clear the avalanche of cardboard, wrappers and ice cream sticks that were strewn everywhere. The prize, of course, was leftovers – Ismail handed them the trays and watched with pleasure as the urchins polished off every last scrap.

* * * * *

Everything changed one July evening. Ismail had just closed the sweet shop. He had kicked off his slippers and was leaning against the doorway, waiting for the urchins to lick the trays clean. His muslin cloth hung over one shoulder. He used the cloth to wipe his hands after handling the sticky sweets and, as usual, the towel had acquired the heavy odours of the day's preparations. A man wearing a red shirt ran by.

"Karachi-wallah!" he screamed at Ismail. "Go back to Pakistan!"

The man pulled back his hand to throw something and Ismail instinctively crisscrossed his arms across his face. He heard the crash of splintering glass. It was followed by the sound of running footsteps. When Ismail uncovered his face, the first thing he noticed was the frightened look of the street children. Glass from the broken window display lay scattered everywhere. Ismail looked down. Tiny shimmering slivers surrounded his bare feet.

"Fetch the brooms," he commanded flatly. "Sweep the glass."

The urchins didn't move. He repeated the command, but

they continued to stare at him and Ismail realised they were not listening. They gaped at him with shocked fascination. He examined his forearms. There were patches of red spreading over his sleeves. He touched his face. His fingers came away stained with blood. He felt no pain. He daubed his face with the muslin cloth. The blood came from somewhere above his right eye. He lifted the towel to his face again and the crimson accumulated. The cloth coated his wound with sugar and sticky syrup. The urchins were still wide-eyed.

"What are you staring at?" he shouted at the nearest one. The boy, who was about twelve, startled and dropped a tray on Ismail's foot. The shopkeeper exploded.

"Clumsy fool–!" The shopkeeper lunged for the boy and grabbed his collar. The boy's shirt was several sizes too big. It looked as if Ismail held him in a net.

"I'm sorry, I'm sorry–" The urchin tried to wriggle out of the shirt. Ismail swiftly let go of the cloth and snatched the boy's wrist. The urchin looked at his trapped hand and began to cry.

A crowd collected outside the shop. The sound of shattering glass had been heard all the way down the street.

"Teach him a good lesson," someone yelled.

"Is this how the bastard repays so much kindness?"

"Hit him, brother!"

Ismail looked up, confused.

"Why do you stop?" one shouted.

"The window will cost at least two thousand rupees."

Ismail let go of the boy's wrist. The urchin refused to run away, now fearing the crowd more than the shopkeeper. He cried without making a sound.

A police constable pushed his way to the front of the crowd.

"Brother, what happened?"

"The glass is broken–" Ismail responded vaguely.

"I'm glad you caught him." The constable was a large fellow with a very thin moustache. Ismail knew him well. He had been a customer for years. He had a fondness for carrot halwa. The policeman brandished his bamboo truncheon.

"No, no …" Ismail began. "Actually–"

The policeman took a swipe at the boy. The heavy stick made a cracking sound as it hit the urchin's knee. The boy screamed in agony.

"Have you been inside the lock-up?" the policeman shouted. " We know how to look after fellows like you."

Now it was the boy who clung to Ismail.

"It wasn't him," the shopkeeper said.

"There's no need for you to protect him, brother," the policeman said.

A voice from the crowd shouted, "You have too kind a heart, Ismail."

"We saw him do it," another voice said.

Ismail felt a strange taste in his mouth. He wiped his face

and realised that blood was streaming down his cheek. The shop spun.

"You had better go to the doctor," the constable told Ismail, as he leaned over and took hold of the boy's arm.

"Tell them. Please tell them." The boy's face was contorted in fear. He clung desperately to Ismail.

"Shut up, you bastard!" the policeman shouted. "I'll teach you to talk nonsense like that."

"Wait," said Ismail with an effort. "It wasn't him at all. It was a man wearing a red shirt who shouted that I should go back to Pakistan."

The crowd hushed. People glanced at each other and began to slip away. The policeman's face became expressionless. Blood dripped off Ismail's face and fell onto his shirt.

*   *   *   *   *

The word pounded in Ismail's skull as he slipped home. He stopped by a clinic on the way and a doctor put in seven stitches above his eye and bandages on his forearms.

He eased the front door open, afraid that his bloodied body would frighten Nasreen and Abid. There were voices from the drawing room. Nasreen was having one of her soirees. Ismail went to the kitchen and poured himself a glass of cold lassi. He held the glass to his cheek, sat down at the dining table and closed his eyes. Karachi-wallah, Karachi-wallah, the man from Karachi. What had he meant? Who was the red-shirted fellow?

Ismail had never seen Karachi in his life. He was born in Bangalore, had grown up in the city. So had his parents and his extended family. He had not the slightest curiosity about any place outside Bangalore, let alone any desire to visit Pakistan. Why had the man picked him out for attack? Ismail instinctively knew the answer, but he instinctively rejected it, too. The man had attacked him because he was Muslim. But that made no sense. He was hardly religious. When Muslim customers talked about Islam, he simply assumed a grave expression and nodded. The rising cost of sugar was more important to him than anything the mullahs said.

The hubbub from the dining room rose and fell. There was laughter and the sound of clinking glasses. Ismail paid no attention. The discussions at Nasreen's soirees made as much sense to him as the talk of the mullahs: Had Pakistani scientists really tried to steal India's monsoon rains? What were the socio-economic consequences of the ongoing border war with Pakistan? Who cared? Ismail poured himself another lassi. What was he to do? Would there be more attacks? Would there be attacks on Nasreen and Abid? What if Abid was standing in the doorway when the red-shirted man came by with a flaming torch? Ismail choked. He clenched his fists. An unbearable, overwhelming surge of protectiveness swept over him. It would never happen, he swore, he would make sure that would never—

"Father?" Abid appeared in the kitchen doorway.

"Abid, son —" Ismail began, struggling out of his chair. "I'm all right. It's just a small cut—"

Abid displayed no trace of surprise or shock.

"I got hurt," Ismail said in a quieter voice, taken aback by his son's composure.

"They got you, too."

Ismail heard Abid's last word almost before it was spoken. Too? Too?

"Abidullah! My child, my son, what happened?" Ismail reached to embrace his son but Abid drew back.

"Nothing. I'm fine."

"Too, you said, 'too,'" Ismail insisted. "What happened. Tell me, tell me."

"I'm fine."

"The bastards, I'll kill the bastards, tell me what happened—?"

Abid sized up Ismail's wounds, as if he was making an inventory.

"It's nothing," he said. "I've just been hearing things, that's all."

"What things?"

"The usual. College-talk. Hindu-Muslim. Go back to Pakistan. How did you get hurt?"

Ismail did not hear Abid's question. He collapsed into his chair. The *usual?*

"How long has this been going on?" he asked finally.

Abid shrugged with the practiced nonchalance of a twenty-year-old.

"Sixty years."

*   *   *   *   *

Ismail sat late at a window, staring at the front street. Could there be more danger in the night? The red-shirted man was unlikely to attack again so soon. Ismail replayed the evening's attack, but there was nothing to it, the whole thing had lasted a few seconds. And through much of it, he had closed his eyes and shielded his face.

Nasreen had been frightened and sympathetic, but unhelpful about what to do. Her friends had trooped into the kitchen on learning that Ismail had been attacked. A man named Lakshman Murthy, whom Ismail vaguely recognised from a recent article in the *Bangalore Times*, said the attack proved that fundamentalism was on the rise. Others talked about secularism and nationalism. Ismail resented every one of them. All they wanted to do was attach a label to what had happened, as if that would make any difference. What was he going to do? Who could he turn to for help?

In the morning he would talk to the police and see about getting some security. It wasn't the attack itself that was as scary as what the red-shirted man had said. He wanted Ismail out, out of the store, out of Bangalore, out of the country. Even if he agreed to leave, where was he to go? How did you change countries? It wasn't as though he had friends or relatives in Pakistan who would take him in. He didn't have a passport, he had never thought of living in any place other than Bangalore.

The police, yes that was it. The police would help. The night constables would include Ismail's street as part of their patrol. But what about the times that the police were not within shouting distance? The red-shirted man could easily hide until the nightly patrol had come and gone. Ismail fingered the stitches over his eye. He would get a security guard to keep watch at night. And what about the shop? And what about his daily walk to and from the shop, a good mile? And what about guarding Nasreen and Abid when they left the house? What about Sundays and the days the security guard was sick? Was he to get bodyguards to follow them twenty-four hours a day? Not even the Prime Minister and the President had security like that. What then?

He had to learn to defend himself. A gun. Ismail startled. A gun? The evening had muddied his head. Of course he wasn't going to get a gun. Only gangsters and idiots did things like that. It wasn't in his nature to carry a gun, let alone use it. But what else was there to do? Was he to sit back and let himself be attacked again? He remembered there was a pistol somewhere in the house, a family heirloom. He hadn't seen it for fifteen years, not since the time he had used it to make Abid laugh as he fired blanks in the air.

Ismail put on his slippers and headed towards the small room where the family's accumulated junk was stored: Boxes, receipts, old toys, clothes, broken furniture, newspapers with headlines about the assassinations of Prime Ministers, cobwebs, dust and pests. It would be difficult to find the gun in the dark, but he had to do it while Nasreen and Abid were asleep. They would be terrified to know he had armed himself – they would understand the true extent of the danger. And bullets. He had to buy bullets. He would have to find out who sold things like that.

He reached for the knob and found the door to the storage room was already ajar. Puzzled, Ismail pursed his lips. A furrow appeared on his forehead. He pushed the door open and it creaked and the figure who stood inside whirled around and the fear caught in Ismail's throat and he began to scream and then he stopped.

It was Abid. Ismail's heart pounded. In the faint light, Ismail could see the glint of white in his son's eyes and another glint from the object he held in his hands. Father and son stood motionless, each waiting for the other to acknowledge what he was doing. It was Abid who acted first. He put the pistol into his pocket and edged past Ismail. The shopkeeper's chest heaved and his hands trembled. He stood like that for a long time. Then he quietly pulled the door shut and crept away to bed.

* * * * *

In the morning, Ismail put two thousand rupees for the bullets into an old envelope and slipped it beneath the door of Abid's bedroom. Then he dressed and went to the police station. An Inspector received him.

"Good morning," Ismail said. "I wanted to talk to you about an incident last night."

The Inspector had a powerful build. His shoulders and chest filled out his shirt, and his lapel was covered with medals and ribbons. Directly behind him was a large framed photograph of Lord Shiva with a cobra wrapped around his blue neck. On the desk were photographs of the Inspector's children. A bronze nameplate was turned towards Ismail. It read: A.M. Madhukar.

"I need to file a report," Ismail said.

The Inspector looked at him, expressionless.

"What kind of report?"

"So you can start an investigation."

"What kind of an investigation?"

"My shop was attacked last night. The man who attacked my shop wore a red shirt."

Inspector Madhukar blinked. Apart from his eyelids, his body was as still as a statue.

"He broke my shop's glass display with a rock," Ismail went on hurriedly. "He shouted, he shouted—"

The shopkeeper could not bring himself to repeat the red-shirted man's words.

"I need protection, my family needs police protection. A night patrol and a constable near the shop and—"

Inspector Madhukar remained perfectly still. Ismail felt the blood rush to his face.

"What did this man shout?" The Inspector's voice was level, as expressionless as his features.

"He told me to go away," Ismail whispered. "Back to Pakistan."

Inspector Madhukar stared at Ismail unwaveringly. There was something in his eyes – disbelief? Or was it pity? – and it made Ismail afraid.

"I've never been to Pakistan in my life," Ismail said. He sounded apologetic. "He called me, 'Karachi-wallah.' I've never been to Karachi. I don't know anyone in Karachi. I need protection. Police protection."

The Inspector picked up a pen and turned it around slowly.

"That won't be necessary," he said in his flat voice. "We have a full confession from the boy."

"What boy?"

"The urchin who was responsible for the incident."

"But that's impossible. That boy is innocent. He's barely twelve. He would never do a thing like that. I know him well – I told the constable last night."

"Perhaps you were in too great a shock to realise that the boy was responsible."

"No! I saw the man who was responsible. He came running up the street. Other people must have seen him running away. You have to open an investigation."

"I cannot do that. The case has already been closed. The guilty have been punished."

Ismail's head reeled. "Punished? How can you punish an innocent child?"

"He is neither innocent nor a child. He has been responsible for other incidents as well."

"You found him guilty without asking me to give you a positive identification?"

"He made out a full confession. I heard it myself last night. You have no need for police protection. Nobody is going to attack you again. You have nothing to worry about."

"Where is the boy?" Ismail asked. "Let me talk to him

and I will show you that he is innocent."

"I am not able to disclose that information." Inspector Madhukar rose to his feet and held out his hand.

Ismail stood up, too. "Don't you understand?" he said. "The boy would never do a thing like that."

The Inspector towered a full head over Ismail. The shopkeeper limply took the officer's outstretched hand.

"Be careful," the Inspector said in his expressionless voice. "Times are bad. You can't trust anyone."

*　*　*　*　*

Ismail closed his shop while the glass window display was being replaced. Customers who dropped by offered their commiserations.

"Terrible, terrible."

"The city is going to the dogs."

"Where are the police when you need them?"

Ismail responded warily to all the comments. He had taken Inspector Madhukar's advice to heart. He watched the faces, to see if anyone appeared satisfied at the destruction. He tried to spot the red-shirted man. It was no use. In the first hour, he identified six different people who might have been the assailant. He had simply not got a good look at the man.

The new display window cost four thousand rupees. Ismail had the workmen put in a new padlock and install fluorescent lights that brightly illuminated the street. That was another two thousand. He knew his security measures were puny. The neighbourhood was a patchwork of tiny streets, alleys and byways that sometimes ran through private houses. Homes and shops were crowded together. The same congestion that had made the spot ideal for commerce now made it impossible to defend. An attacker could slip in and out through any of a dozen alleys. He could lob a flaming torch from a neighbouring rooftop. In the evening rush, he could leave a suitcase with a time bomb in the corner and no one would notice it ...

Karachi-wallah, Karachi-wallah, Karachi-wallah. The man from Karachi.

Ismail asked the men to put up a new signboard. When he opened the sweet shop three decades ago, he had painted a signboard himself: Ismail Ahmed Sweets. It had rusted long ago and the letters were indecipherable. Ismail's fame sufficed to draw customers to the shop. Word of mouth was how people found their way to him. Now he wanted a neutral, non-Muslim name: "Bangalore Sweets." What could be safer than naming the business after the city? The workers grumbled at the extra work and Ismail had to pay them a premium. As the signboard was being painted, a man in a white robe appeared. He wore the cap of the devout on his head. The workers greeted him respectfully. Ismail recognised him as a leader at the local mosque. The shopkeeper kept his distance – if the red-shirted man or any of his friends was secretly watching, he did not want to give the impression that he was the friend of a mullah. Ismail, the mullah and the workmen stood in a loose semi-circle and watched the paint dry.

"Bangalore sweets," the mullah said, with a smile that revealed two missing teeth. He was a short man with a stubby beard.

Ismail nodded.

"A good name," the religious leader continued, but there was the hint of mockery in his voice.

Ismail did not respond. The mullah touched his arm. "A word in private, brother."

"Some other time. I'm busy now."

"There may not be another time."

The smile disappeared from the mullah's face. He squeezed Ismail's arm. The workmen shuffled their feet and pretended not to listen. Ismail was taken aback at the mullah's insolence but did not want to make a scene.

"I'll only be gone a minute," he told the workmen. "Nail the sign so that it catches the light."

He led the mullah into the shop.

"My name is Qasim. I lead afternoon prayers at the mosque on—"

"I know who you are. What can I do for you?"

The man touched Ismail's sleeve again. "Impatience, brother, such impatience."

"I have many things on my mind. There is a great deal for me to worry about."

"That is why I have come. All of us need God's help in times of trouble."

The mullah's bland smile had returned. Ismail saw that it

was a trick of the lips, the man's eyes lacked all humour. The mullah's features were just as inscrutable as Inspector Madhukar's, his manner just as expressionless.

"I'm not in trouble," Ismail said. "There was just a bad incident last night, that's all. Everything is cleared up now."

"With God's help, such things won't happen again."

"I don't think God can be of much help."

"Well, perhaps His followers can be of assistance then."

"I don't know what you mean. If you will excuse me—"

"Why do you reject the hand of your friends, my brother? I could offer you help. If you had the courage to openly stand with me in the street, people would respect you more. Nobody would dare to attack your shop. They would be afraid to be your enemies."

"I don't have any enemies."

The mullah's smile broadened. "Have it your way, brother. You have no enemies. But times are bad. We all need friends."

"I'm a businessman," Ismail said shortly. "If I need protection, I will go to the police and they will—"

The shopkeeper faltered and Qasim pounced.

"Yes brother, they will what? You've gone to them already, haven't you? Have they promised you an armed guard twenty-four hours a day?"

Ismail was silent.

"Did you speak to Inspector Madhukar? Ah yes, I see

you recognise the name. You needn't tell me what he said, I already know. Brother, I am the eyes and ears of the faithful in this community. I know many people who have gone to Inspector Madhukar. Sometimes he promises help, if the person is influential. And then the policeman is missing during the hour of the next attack. Otherwise, he says the case is solved and the guilty have been apprehended and punished."

Ismail reached out and placed a hand on a wall to steady himself.

"I can understand your fear, brother," the mullah continued. "You do not come to prayers, so you do not know what is happening in the community. You do not know what your brothers face, day in and day out. You are wealthy and you believe that money can protect you. But that is an illusion, brother. Only faith can protect you, faith and the faithful. Everyone understands this except you. Even your son."

"Abid?" Ismail choked on the word. "You know Abid?"

"I know him like a son. I have often wished that he were really my son. I do not know anyone so intelligent, so faithful, so brave—"

"Leave Abid out of this," Ismail said, trying to summon up all the authority he could muster. "You want money? I'll pay you money, but leave my son alone."

The mullah looked at Ismail steadily. He touched the shopkeeper's arm.

"Keep your money," he said softly. "I came to ask you for your faith. I see that I have failed. But God is great and he has many ways of bringing the faithful to his fold."

The mullah raised one arm in salute and walked away.

*   *   *   *   *

Nasreen handed Ismail a sheet of paper when he returned home. It was a letter-to-the-editor that she had composed about religious intolerance. He read it because he didn't have the heart to tell her it was a puny gesture. Words, words, words. What were words but wasted breath and wasted ink? The people who threw firebombs didn't read the letters to the editor.

"Dear Sir," she had written. "There has been a spate of religious intolerance because of the border war with Pakistan. There are some Indians who seem to think that all Muslims are disloyal to India. This has led to the ludicrous spectacle of various communities trying to outdo each other in patriotism. Last week, elderly Muslim leaders offered to go to the war front to fight the Pakistanis. Tomorrow, Muslim school children will offer to fight. Just this week, our family business was attacked by a man who warned us to return to Pakistan. When will all this madness end? Yours sincerely, Nasreen Ahmed."

"When are you going to mail it?" asked Ismail.

"One of the people in my group knows an editor at the *Bangalore Times* and will come by tonight to pick it up. Madan Doha Singh—he was here last night. The tall fellow with glasses."

Ismail did not remember Madan Singh. "I hope they publish it," he said.

The telephone rang. Ismail answered. The caller had a deep voice.

"Karachi-wallah. Have you finished packing your bags?"

Ismail's face went pale. "Who is speaking?"

Nasreen made a gesture to ask who it was. Ismail turned his back to her.

The voice on the phone said, "You think a new shop sign will save you? We won't know it is still you standing behind the counter? Sister-fucker, you think we are fools?"

"No, please. I didn't—"

"Twenty-four hours, you circumcised bastard. We give you twenty-four hours to take your wife and your son and go back to Pakistan."

The line went dead. Ismail pressed it tightly to his ear. "Sorry, wrong number," he said into the silence.

He turned to Nasreen. "It was a wrong number."

She stared at him disbelievingly.

He clenched and unclenched his fists. His neck was a knot of angry muscle.

"About the letter —" he said finally. "Maybe it would be better if you didn't sign your name. Why not write, 'a concerned citizen?'

Abid appeared in the doorway. He wore a flowing white shirt and a skullcap.

"Papa, I'm going for evening prayers. Will you come, too?"

Nasreen's jaw dropped at Abid's attire.

"What do you think you're doing?" she asked. "That's

not funny. Just because we are not religious doesn't mean we should make fun–"

Abid looked steadily at his father. Ismail could not remember the last time he had seen his son go to the mosque.

"Papa, are you coming?"

"Yes," Ismail said, surprising himself. "I'll get dressed."

He left the room before Nasreen could say anything. As he hunted for his cap, he heard his wife and son argue.

"Why are you going to the mosque?"

"It's high time we got to know our people."

"Our people? Since when did we need to go to the mosque to meet our people?"

"Throughout history."

"Have you gone mad?"

"No, I have finally become sane."

Ismail came back into the room.

"Why are you going, too?" Nasreen asked. "You don't even believe in God."

"I do now," he replied. "God has many ways of bringing the faithful to his fold."

*   *   *   *   *

They walked, side by side. Ismail was both frightened for and proud of his son. There was so much about Abid that he didn't know. Overnight, he had become his own person; he had become a man. Their roles had switched. It was he who now needed Abid's advice.

"Abid," the shopkeeper said. "The man who attacked me called just now."

"What did he say?"

"He said we have twenty-four hours to return to Pakistan."

"Qasim," said Abid finally. "We must tell Qasim. He will know what to do."

More and more men emerged from the alleys and byways. They adjusted their caps and joined the procession towards the mosque. The road ahead was crowded with the faithful, and the crowd swelled behind them. Our people, Abid had said. Our people. My people, Ismail thought. Hundreds of men, men who would be ready to defend each other, men who would defend him. Faith and the faithful, that was what Qasim had said, faith and the faithful would come to the rescue. With each passing step, Ismail felt safer than he had ever felt. Why had he been obstinate so long?

Around him were labourers and merchants, college professors and artisans. All wore the same clothes, no one was high and no one was low. All had the same prayers and God would hear them all equally. Father and son stepped inside the cool darkness of the mosque. All around, the faithful greeted each other, raised cupped fingers to their chins.

And in the forefront, Ismail glimpsed Qasim. The mullah scanned the rows of the faithful, and it seemed as if his eyes rested a moment on Ismail, and it seemed as if he smiled.

* * * * *

There were five men in the little room with Ismail and Abid. Besides Qasim, Ismail did not recognise any of them. Abid appeared relaxed in their company.

"What did the telephone caller say?" Qasim asked.

"He told me to go back to Pakistan," said Ismail agitatedly. "He said painting a new signboard would not save me. Twenty-four hours. He gave me twenty-four hours to pack up and leave. Where am I to go? I do not have anywhere to—"

"Enough, brother," Qasim said shortly. "By coming to prayers today you have given up the person you were before. The faithful do not tremble when the enemy rattles his sword. The faithful have no fear."

"I have a wife and child—"

"Your wife is secular," said Qasim, delivering the word with contempt. "Nobody will harm her. These people want all Muslims to be like your wife, renouncing religion and retribution, answering force with puny words. They know it would castrate us, divide brother from brother, and then they can destroy us because we would have lost the sword of our faith and the shield of the faithful."

Ismail wanted to say that he had been secular, too, in the sense that he hadn't cared one way or another about religion. But he was too amazed at the extent to which Qasim knew about his family. Had Abid told him all this?

"And about your son," Qasim continued, "you have nothing to fear about your son. He is more than capable of looking after his own safety. He is more than capable of looking after you, for that matter. He is one of the jewels of this community."

The boy showed no reaction to Qasim's praise and neither did any of the other men, as if Abid's bravery was a proven thing, an agreed-upon fact. Ismail wondered when his son had found the time to help the community? And what did this help involve? His college report cards had always been excellent. He had friends, played cricket and went to watch movies. Where did he find time for anything else in such a packed schedule?

The other men in the room began to speak: "The threats are increasing, Qasim. We have to act."

"Four brothers have been arrested. We have not heard from them since."

"What do our brothers in the police department say?" asked Qasim.

"They are silent," the man replied. "Many of them are being transferred, one of them has been suspended. We have had no information from them in more than a week."

"Why are the attacks increasing now?" asked Ismail.

"The border war with Pakistan provides a cover," replied Qasim. "The attacks can be justified in the name of national security. The police have unprecedented powers, the courts are silenced. This is what they have wanted to do for sixty years."

Sixty years. Abid had said that, too. Had he been blind these many years that he had not seen these undercurrents? The sweet shop had been prosperous and he had been content and he had not thought about anyone or anything else.

"Qasim, we must respond," one of the other men said. "The longer we are silent, the more they will believe that we are weak."

"Offence is the best defence," said another man.

"Do not delay, Qasim. In a few weeks, we will all be behind bars, arrested on false charges. You will not have the weapons you have now. They will remove your limbs, one by one, and then they will come for you and you will be helpless."

Qasim's eyes flashed.

"Helpless? Helpless? You think that if you are taken away from me, I shall be helpless? You forget that my strength does not come from you, it comes from God. Faith is my strength. I shall never be helpless."

"Forgive me, brother," the man replied. "You are right. We trust in God. He will defend us. But there are others who do not have your faith, Qasim. There are hundreds in the community –" the man glanced pointedly at Ismail, "who lack the depth of your faith. Think about them. They depend on you to defend them. We must act now."

Qasim rose and paced the little room.

"It is not a decision to be made lightly," he said, speaking so softly that Ismail wasn't sure if he was just thinking aloud. "Once we embark on that road, there is no turning back."

"We are already embarked on that road."

"There is already no turning back."

"Things are dire, Qasim. If we hesitate, all will be lost."

Qasim paced some more. Finally, to Ismail's amazement, he turned to Abid.

"What do you think, Abidullah? The others are rash, but

you know how to think before you act. What is your opinion?"

Abid showed no sign of discomfiture. All the men in the room listened attentively–Ismail realised they had done this before. When had his twenty-year-old developed the maturity to command such respect? Pride and fear battled inside Ismail's heart. Did they realise that he was only a child? He was talented and gifted, but he was only a boy.

"We must act, but not indiscriminately," said Abid, in a voice so level that it sent shivers down Ismail's spine. "We need to send them a message."

"What kind of a message?" Qasim asked.

"We need to show them what we are capable of doing. We need to show them that we are not afraid. We need to strike back."

"An anonymous telephone call!" exclaimed Ismail. "A call that would frighten them the same way they frightened me."

Qasim and the others regarded Ismail without saying anything. Qasim turned again to Abid:

"What are you saying?"

"Inspector Madhukar," said Abid.

*   *   *   *   *

"My husband," said Nasreen, introducing Ismail to Madan Singh. Her voice was icy, she was clearly embarrassed by his attire. Ismail had just returned from the mosque.

They shook hands. Madan Singh looked barely older than Abid. Ismail wondered what Qasim would think if he knew that Nasreen had been entertaining a young man at home while her husband was at prayers.

"I came to pick up the letter from your wife," said Madan Singh, speaking in a thin voice that was inflected with stray high pitches.

"The letter to the editor," added Nasreen.

"Did you do what I asked?" Ismail asked her.

"No," said Nasreen. "I've decided to sign it."

Her eyes dared him to have an argument with her in Madan Singh's presence.

"It's the best thing," said Madan Singh. "We talked about your concerns and Nasreen and I decided there was no reason to be afraid. She is a citizen and she has the right to speak her mind. It's a constitutional right."

Nasreen and I. Nasreen and I decided. Madan Singh knew Nasreen well. How long had he been coming to her soirees?

"Justice and the courts will protect you," said Madan Singh. "I'm a final year law student. If there is trouble, we can file a brief and get a restraining order imposed on anyone who threatens you."

Justice and the courts. Did they sound at all like faith and the faithful? The shield of justice and the sword of the courts. No, it didn't sound right. Not when the police were themselves thugs. Madan Singh and Nasreen had no idea of the kind of world they were dealing with, stuck as they were with their letters to the editor and their restraining orders.

Ismail looked Madan Singh in the eye. "This is a private family matter. It would be better if you did not interfere."

"Ismail!" Nasreen's voice was shocked. "Madan is a friend. How could you say such a thing?"

"Well friend," said Ismail to Madan Singh, "In friendship, I ask you not to interfere."

Madan Singh's face flushed. He stiffly handed the letter to Ismail. "I should get going. Good night."

He did not wait for a response. He nodded once at Nasreen and walked out. Nasreen wheeled on Ismail.

"How dare you—"

"Enough." He held up an index finger. "There is much you do not know. We are in more danger than you think. The telephone caller in the evening was the same man who attacked me. He warned us he would attack again within twenty-four hours."

Her face drained of colour. "I knew it, I knew it, I knew that something had happened."

"I have taken precautionary measures," Ismail said, walking to the bedroom. "Things will get better soon."

"I don't care about myself," she called after him. "It's Abid I'm worried about."

He turned at the door.

"He is more than capable of looking after himself. He is more than capable of looking after all of us. He is one of the jewels of this community."

*   *   *   *   *

After dinner, Ismail tiptoed to Abid's room. The door was ajar and the light was on. Normally, Ismail would enter without knocking, but now he hesitated. He tapped on the door.

"Yes?"

Ismail pushed the door open. Clothes and CDs were strewn over the bed. Posters of cricket stars hung on the walls. Abid was sitting at his desk. He held a pencil in one hand and supported his forehead with the other. A table lamp shone over his shoulder and there were textbooks and papers scattered before him. The model student.

"Son, Abid, I was wondering if there was any help I could give you."

"I'm preparing for a calculus exam tomorrow."

"I didn't mean your studies. The other thing, what you said back at prayers with Qasim."

Abid smiled faintly. "I don't think I need any help there either. Qasim is going to plan everything."

"What is there to plan? All you need is a telephone in a public place where the call cannot be traced."

"It's all for Qasim to decide. He makes all the decisions. He will take care of everything."

"But if you make the call from our home, they might be able to trace it."

"No," said Abid slowly. "I won't make any calls from the house."

A dark fear grew at the back of Ismail's mind. "It is a telephone call that you are planning, isn't it?" he asked.

Abid showed no annoyance at his father's persistence. "What else can it be?"

"Has Qasim told you to place a muffler over the phone – a shawl or something – to make your voice sound different?"

"That's a good idea."

"It would make more sense for one of the others to make the call, though. Their voices are deeper and will be harder to identify."

"Most of them are being watched."

"You will be careful, won't you?"

"I'll be very careful. And Qasim will make sure all our plans have back-up options. Don't worry about it. Now, I must study for this exam."

"Yes, of course." Ismail toyed with the doorknob. "I realise I was hasty this morning when I dropped off an envelope with money. And last night–"

"You're absolutely right," replied Abid evenly. "I put the envelope back in your drawer."

"Oh, good. That's good. After all, the best weapons are faith and the faithful."

"Yes," said Abid. "Faith and the faithful."

Nasreen was lying in bed when Ismail got to the darkened bedroom. He knew she was awake because she lay stiff, whereas when she was asleep her breathing made soft, regular sounds. He lay down beside her and placed his hands behind his head. He could feel her eyes on him in the dark.

"Why did you go to prayers today?" Her voice was so close to his ear that he startled, even though he knew they were about to have a conversation.

"We all need friends in times of trouble," Ismail replied.

"We go to the police in times of trouble. Why have you brainwashed Abid? Why did you get him involved?"

Ismail said nothing. If anything, it was Abid who had brainwashed him. Nasreen would not understand. She had grown up in the company of educated people, whereas everyone in his family had made their living working with their hands. She did not have a feel for life on the streets, her soirees were filled with people like Madan Singh. Were any of them devout? Did they understand the security that came with being with one's own people, the faithful? What could they know of the ways of the street?

He heard a short, sharp intake of breath. She was crying. He turned over on his side and patted her cheek. It was glistening with tears. "Everything will be all right," he said.

"Everything won't be all right. You think you know what you are doing, but you are in over your head. And now you have taken our son away. You talk to him and your voices are hushed, because I must not hear what you are saying. Ismail,

Ismail, if you won't let me help, why don't you at least leave Abid out of this?"

"I haven't got Abid into anything."

"You're telling me that he is the one who is leading you?" she asked wryly.

Ismail bit his lip in the dark. Maybe he should have explained everything to her from the start. But now it was too late. So much had happened. She would never understand the chain of events. She pulled her cheek away from under his hand and turned her back on him.

"I don't care what you do, but please leave Abid out of this," she said.

"I haven't asked him to do anything."

"Promise me."

"I promise."

*   *   *   *   *

The next morning, when Ismail emerged from his morning shower, there were no fresh clothes and no clean muslin cloth waiting for him. He stared at the blank bed in astonishment. Nasreen had performed the ritual so many thousands of times that Ismail had come to regard it as a natural phenomenon, incapable of change.

He dressed himself and draped an old cloth over his shoulder. He found Nasreen in the living room. She was sitting at the dining table and her head was in her hands. She was wearing only a nightgown and there were deep furrows across her forehead. Strands of grey hair fell across her eyes.

"What's the matter?" asked Ismail. "You tossed and turned all night. You were so restless that I couldn't sleep, either. And this morning, my clothes, the muslin cloth – I told you that everything would be all right. Don't you believe me?"

She looked at him through unfocussed eyes.

"Nasreen, did you hear what I said?"

Her lips opened and closed soundlessly. With great effort she said, "Abid."

Ismail rubbed the muslin across his face. It did not have the newly washed smell he so liked. "What about Abid? I promised you, didn't I? I told you I wouldn't get him involved."

"He's gone." She spoke without malice, anger or fear.

"Gone where?"

She shrugged.

"He's probably gone to college," said Ismail. "He had a calculus exam today."

"The college is closed," she replied. "It's in all the papers. They've declared it a Victory Day holiday."

"Victory day?"

"India defeated Pakistan."

For a fleeting half-second, Ismail wasn't sure whether Nasreen was talking about a cricket match. "The border war," he said softly. "It's over. Maybe Abid didn't hear it was a holiday and went to college?"

"He cleaned his room before he left. Does anyone spend two hours before an examination cleaning their room?"

Ismail went to Abid's room. The bedcovers were neatly folded and there was not a stray shirt or CD in sight. The desk was immaculately organised. The wood glistened as if it had been polished and the windowsills were free of dust. There was something else that was odd. The walls. The cricket posters had vanished. In their place stood a single framed picture of thousands of white-clothed men touching their foreheads to the ground at the annual Hajj prayers in Mecca.

Ismail fingered the frame. It was expensive and hand-carved. Where had Abid found the money to buy such a finely crafted piece? There was an inscription at the bottom. "For my jewel, Abidullah. Your spiritual father, Qasim."

There was a step behind him. Nasreen entered the room.

"Do you know who Qasim is?" she asked.

"No." He tried to keep his expression impassive.

"Ismail, we need to do something," she said, placing a hand on his shoulder. "Our son needs us. Needs us both."

"What do you want to do?"

"What does any citizen do when their child disappears? We go to the police."

"No!" He shrugged her hand off with a violent shudder. "No police. We leave the police out of this. They are nothing but thugs and crooks—"

"What has got into you? Are you crazy?"

"I said, no police. We can't go to the police."

"Ismail, tell me what's going on?" Her voice was almost a scream.

"Nothing's going on. Listen Nasreen, we are overreacting. We don't know that anything is wrong. Abid may have gone to college because he didn't know it was a holiday. He may have cleaned his room before he left. That's not enough reason to go to the police. They will laugh at you. What are you going to say? "I need to open an investigation because my son has cleaned his room?""

The muslin cloth fell off his shoulder and he stooped to pick it up. He saw a flash of white under the bed, a sheet of paper. Was it a stray sheet that Abid had missed while cleaning? Or was it a message to his parents, meant to be discovered later? Ismail straightened and faced Nasreen. Whatever it was, he did not want her to see it.

"What should we do?" she asked.

"Why don't you wait in the living room?" he suggested. "Let me go and see if Abid is at the mosque. If he has not returned by the time I'm back, we'll think of something to do."

Her face went pale. "Our son is missing and you want to waste time at the mosque?"

"Nasreen, if Abid is in trouble, it is God who can save our son."

He left the room and hoped she would follow him out. She did not. He put on his prayer cap and slipped out of the house. Faith and the faithful. He was keeping his faith. Would the faithful now stand by him? He needed Qasim. He had placed all his store by this man. If anything happened to Abid – no, he would not even think it. Qasim was a good planner. He would have made backup plans. Abid was on a mission and he would return safely. There was nothing to do but wait. Nasreen had unnecessarily shaken him up. Abid was the jewel of the community. Qasim had said so himself. Nothing would go wrong. Nothing could go wrong. But how long did it take to make a telephone call? Ismail remembered Abid's expression the previous evening. Perhaps it was not a telephone call. Perhaps Abid had meant something more violent. Ismail hurried faster.

It was early for the next prayer session. Ismail slipped into the mosque and scanned the faces, looking for Qasim or one of the other men from the previous day's meeting. He asked an old man sitting on a bench where he could find Qasim. The man waved him towards an inner room.

Ismail knocked on the door. There was no response. He knocked harder and finally banged on it with his open palm. It opened a crack and an eye peered out at him. Ismail thought he recognised one of the men from the previous day.

"What is it?"

"Brother, I'm looking for Qasim."

The eye scanned Ismail from head to toe.

"Qasim is not here."

"I need to ask him about my son, Abid, Abidullah. When is Qasim going to be back?"

"In an hour or two."

"I'll wait for him here. Is that all right?"

The man did not answer. He closed the door and shot the bolt.

Ismail sat down on the bench beside the old man. The man did not react. He stared into space in the way that blind people do. Ismail buried his head in his hands.

The minutes passed and the mosque began to fill with men. Ismail wondered whether to return home, but he did not want to face Nasreen until he had heard from Qasim. He knelt on a prayer mat with the others. Someone he did not recognise led the prayers. When it was over, Ismail sat beside the old man again. He had not eaten breakfast or lunch and he felt light-headed. What was the message in the note under Abid's bed? Where was Qasim? Ismail knocked on the door once more but no one answered. By late afternoon, his hunger had disappeared. He banged on the door a last time and the thuds of his palm reverberated through the mosque. No sound came from the room. He stepped outside. His head swam. Would Abid have returned home? Was Qasim's mysterious absence a sign that things had gone wrong? Merciful God, he prayed, have pity on one of your faithful.

The house was quiet when Ismail got home. He opened the front door and let himself in. "Nasreen?" he called. "I'm home. Abid, son, are you back?"

There was silence as he walked through the house. Everything was exactly as he had left it. The chair that Nasreen had sat on in the living room was at the exact angle that he had last seen it. Not a plate or spoon had been moved in the kitchen.

The letter. Abid's note. Ismail went to Abid's room. He switched on the lights and got down on his hands and knees and peered under the bed.

It was gone. A startled cry escaped his lips.

He scanned the desk, threw back the bedcovers, and opened cupboards. He raced to the bathroom. His steps pounded through the house, the living room, the bedroom. He went to the storage room, where Abid had found the gun. He opened boxes and shoved suitcases. Clouds of dust flew into the air and choked him. He coughed and sneezed. Nasreen and Abid. Dearer to him than life itself, dearer than anything. Dearer than faith and the faithful. Where were they?

The phone rang and Ismail jumped. The shrillness was like a siren. He picked up the receiver.

"Hello?"

"Ismail?" A man's voice, familiar, but somehow altered. A man who perhaps was covering the mouthpiece with a piece of cloth.

"Qasim? Qasim, is that you? Abid has not returned—"

Ismail stopped. What if the caller was not Qasim? He bit his tongue and cursed himself. What a fool he was. Had he placed Abid in danger?

"Qasim? You want Qasim?" The man's voice was low. "Karachi-wallah, you thought that swine could save you?"

A chill ran down Ismail's spine.

"I gave you twenty-four hours to leave," the man

continued. "But I've changed my mind. The war is over now. Besides, I admire your wife."

The man laughed.

"Who are you?" Ismail asked.

"She is intelligent and courageous," the voice went on, soliloquising. "She was willing to do anything to defend your son." The voice laughed. "Karachi-wallah, you are a lucky man to have a wife with no inhibitions."

The line went dead.

The telephone spun, the room spun, the house spun. Merciful God, merciful God, what had happened? What had he brought about? Nasreen, beloved wife, Abid, the most precious boy in the world. She must have found Abid's letter and gone in search of him, gone to the police. Had she been molested? Was the voice on the phone baiting him or telling the truth? And where was Abid? He had to go to the police station, he had to claw his way in and save them.

He ran through the house and threw open the front door. Three figures stood outside. Nasreen, Abid and Madan Singh.

The law student had one arm around each of them. Both Nasreen and Abid leaned heavily on him.

Ismail stared at his wife and son. Her sari was crumpled and her hair was askew. She had a vacant look in her eye. There were bruises and scratch marks across her face. Abid looked worse. His shirt was torn in several places and he seemed in pain. He was hunched over and clutching his stomach. He was whimpering.

"Are you all right?" Ismail cried out. "How badly are you hurt?"

"Nasreen sent for me," said Madan Singh.

Ismail felt a dagger go through his heart. He had failed her and she had turned to Madan Singh. Justice and the courts.

"She needed a lawyer," he continued. "I tried to reach you at home, but no one answered the phone."

Ismail helped his wife and son into the house. Madan Singh told him what had happened. Abid had several broken ribs. He had been apprehended near the police station for suspicious behaviour. An ancient pistol had been found in his pocket. He had refused to say what he was doing and had been severely beaten.

"It could have been much worse," said Madan Singh. "Nasreen saved him. But she, she–" He faltered, and his gaze dropped to the floor.

"I did what had to be done," Nasreen said quietly. "It was for us, Ismail, for our child."

Ismail held his wife and son. Hot tears spilled from his eyes.

The Scoop

The train, of course, was late. Collins was nowhere to be seen. Sanjay eyed the rows of cigarette packs in a stall at the railway station and debated whether his resolution to quit applied to out-of-town trips. He bought a pack and leaned against a wall. As he placed a cigarette between his lips, his conscience reminded him that he hadn't yet left Mumbai. He looked at his watch. It wasn't his fault that the train was late. It made no sense to let the vagaries of the Indian railway system limit his pleasures. He lit up, inhaled, and immediately thought of his mother.

"If your father were here –" she had said the week before, spotting an ashtray on his bed. Sanjay's smoking was not a secret, but he tried to be discreet about it at home. She pointedly removed the ashtray, holding it with the tips of two fingers.

"If Dad was here, what?" he had replied, immediately regretting the childish defiance in his voice.

"All this –" The second half sentence took in the untidy desk, the soiled clothes on the floor and the torn posters of film stars. It also took in Sanjay himself, her dead husband and a host of other sorrows that she had borne with patience.

"All right, I'll quit." Sanjay had rolled his eyes and sighed theatrically. He wanted his offer to hurt, as if his one sacrifice could equal all of hers. She had shrugged and left the room.

When he threw his cigarettes away, she showed no gratitude. At the railway station, he inhaled the smoke into his lungs self-righteously. It irritated him that Collins was late. Collins was the photographer, a tall Anglo-Indian with two expanding patches of baldness that almost met at the crown of his head. Collins had worked at the newspaper longer than anyone else, including the senior editors and the maintenance staff. He always projected an exquisite boredom. If the ground had split open before him, swallowing people and automobiles, Collins would have taken a drag from his cigarette, sipped at one of his endless cups of tea, and only then raised his camera. He turned in good work, however, and reporters found that people opened up better during interviews when he was around.

It was thirty-five minutes past the train's scheduled departure when the photographer arrived. Sanjay fixed the older man with a cold stare.

"Did you know the train was late?"

Collins drew on his cigarette. He held it with the tips of his index finger and thumb, as if he was going to write something with it. He slowly shook his head. Smoke dribbled from his lips.

"What if the train had been on time?"

Collins did not reply. What aggravated Sanjay even more was that the train arrived three minutes later. The porters, who squatted on their haunches along the platform, buzzed into activity moments before the train came into view. They were like birds, Sanjay thought, who knew of things to come. The idea pleased him. He made a mental note to include it at some point in his writings.

A porter hoisted their luggage onto his head. Sanjay had

only a small bag with overnight supplies, but Collins had a large suitcase and a smaller bag. They followed the porter to the second class compartment. The man deposited the luggage beneath the small benches and accepted Collins' tip without an argument.

"May God grant that you and the train arrive in Surat together." He grinned and left.

Sanjay thought the man was being insolent, but the humour suited Collins, who laughed. A train crash near Surat the previous week had killed three hundred and fifty-one people. A signalman had held up the wrong lamp.

Sanjay and Collins took the window seats facing each other.

"What's in the suitcase?" Sanjay asked.

Collins popped the locks. There was a small folded tripod and lights, cameras and rolls of film. But most of the space was occupied by a large flag. It was the Indian tricolour, tightly folded. Sanjay could see a bit of the wheel in one corner and the layers of saffron, white and green.

Collins grinned. "Nice shot," he said.

Sanjay nodded although he didn't really understand. One of the first unwritten rules he had learned in the newsroom was that reporters and photographers should keep out of each other's way.

The compartment was heavily overbooked. Men crowded together. The women and children had their own reserved compartment. The crush of bodies made Sanjay uncomfortable.

It was no use complaining to Collins, who seemed unmindful that his shoulder was jammed against the window. The train rocked and moved. Children carrying trays with straps around their necks walked through the train, selling coffee, tea and snacks. Everyone ate, talked and smoked. With the border war against Pakistan in its fifth week, there was only one subject of conversation.

"Two weeks and it will be over."

"Mother-fuckers never learn."

Everyone laughed.

"We had them on their knees in '71."

"We should have taken over."

"We're too trusting."

"That's the problem. We made the same mistake in '65. When are we going to learn?"

"We'll finish them off this time. General Pratap won't spare them."

"He's the right man for the job. He will kill the bastards even if they fall to their knees and beg."

There was a lull. A man sitting beside Sanjay spoke: "What do you do if you have a gun with two bullets and you are in a room with a Pakistani, Hitler and Idi Amin?"

No one knew. There were expectant snickers.

"You shoot the Pakistani twice."

Everyone laughed. It was difficult to guffaw in a space so

cramped, but the joke eased Sanjay's sour mood. That's right, he thought, you shoot the Pakistani twice.

It was Nayak who had given them their current assignment. Nayak was Sanjay's editor, a creative fellow, always brimming with ideas and suggestions. The press release from General Pratap's office had said that the Chief Minister of Gujarat would be visiting the house of a soldier who had been killed in the border war. The war hero was a young man, twenty-two years old. His name, according to the press release, was Corporal Pranlal of the Fourth Indian Rifles Regiment. He had been shot while charging a machine gun nest on a remote mountain peak. He had succeeded too, killing the four intruders who held the peak and then hanging on to life until reinforcements arrived. He died with the words "Hail Mother India" on his lips, the press release concluded, a patriot to the last. The soldier was from Santapur, a small village near Surat. On Saturday, the Chief Minister planned to give the soldier's aging mother, Kamalabehn, a plaque to commemorate her son's service to the nation. The Defence Ministry had followed up the press release with calls to editors of important papers. Although Sanjay's paper was not the most important in Mumbai, General Pratap's assistant, Major Arjun Mishra, had personally called Sanjay's editor: Nayak was immensely pleased about this and immediately agreed to cover the story.

"She's a peasant and she is going to be talking to the Chief Minister," Nayak told Sanjay, jabbing a finger at the press release. "This must be the most important day of her life. Let's get a profile. Go early and talk to her before the Chief Minister arrives. A nice photo. A moving tribute to her son. It'll be a scoop."

Since the start of the border war, Sanjay's newspaper had

consistently won high marks from the Defence Ministry. The newspaper had displayed icons of the Indian flag on the corners of the front page. The paper had set up a war relief fund to compensate the families of fallen soldiers, and dubbed them martyrs. All the columnists were deputed to write about atrocities perpetrated by the Pakistanis and the heroism of Indian soldiers. The paper's war coverage matched the mood of the people and had set it apart from the competition. Circulation was rising. The mood in the newsroom was upbeat. At the daily news meetings, the talk was grave and statesmanlike. Sanjay felt proud to be a reporter. He lingered outside the building before entering each morning so that passing pedestrians would associate him with the most patriotic newspaper in Mumbai.

At Surat, Sanjay and Collins went to the hotel where they were to spend the night. Sanjay dropped a business card at the front desk. The clerk immediately recognised the name of the newspaper. Sanjay felt a sudden gravitas. It pleased him that someone in Surat would instantly identify the name of a newspaper in Mumbai.

"We're here to cover the war effort," he said shortly. "Take us to our room."

The clerk carried the bags himself. He ushered Sanjay and Collins into a room and went about sprucing up the beds and turning on the TV. He clicked his heels to attention and saluted them before leaving. Sanjay stood by the window, smoking. He recalled a photograph he'd seen of President Kennedy at a White House window, gazing into the distance.

Sanjay imagined Pranlal's final minutes. The young soldier

must have volunteered to storm the machine gun nest. He would have set off in the early hours of the morning, under cover of pitch blackness. A slender man in army fatigues, scurrying from crevasse to crevasse, slipping on the snow and ice and gritting his teeth against the bitter wind. A patriot. And then, the machine gun in view, he would have thrown fear aside and run forward, firing and shouting. And then the intruders, the interlopers from Pakistan, would have fired back and the bullets would have struck Pranlal – again and again and again. But they could not stop him. The ridge captured, the Indian soldier must have hung onto life, clenching his fists against the pain. And, as dawn rose over the land he loved, reinforcements would have arrived and Pranlal could finally die, with his country's name on his lips. How had he lived so long with wounds so deep? Love for the motherland is the strongest armour of all. Sanjay felt his throat catch with emotion. He took out his notebook and jotted notes for his story.

They commandeered a taxi and set off for Santapur early the next morning. Sanjay wanted lots of time before the minister and the other journalists arrived. Besides the interview, Collins needed to get a good portrait. The village was set apart from the highway by a dirt road that was pockmarked with potholes. The bouncing taxi churned Sanjay's insides. The press release had given no exact address and when the journalists reached Santapur, they realised why. The village consisted of a maze of mud paths. There were about fifty shacks in all. Chickens, goats and mangy dogs wandered around.

It wasn't hard to find the martyr's home. Outside one of the first shacks, a framed photograph was placed on a chair, adorned with a stringy garland. The young man in the picture looked like a teenager. Sanjay remembered that Pranlal had been just twenty-two. The reporter felt a cold anger against the Pakistanis. Why did this young man have to be cut down on some distant mountain peak, so far from home, so far from hands that could help? And now, the Pakistanis had destroyed not one life but another, a mother who had borne this boy, raised him, nurtured him. Sanjay wished he could drag the killers and their friends and families and show them what they had done.

Two men sat on their haunches outside the shack. Inside, there were sounds of weeping. A curtain was drawn across the entrance. Sanjay gave the older man his business card. This was probably Pranlal's uncle. The man accepted the card as if it was a talisman. He held it reverentially with both hands. Sanjay noticed he was holding it upside down. He seemed in a state of shock.

"We're newspapermen from Mumbai," said Sanjay.

The man nodded uncomprehendingly.

"We want to interview Kamalabehn."

The man said nothing. His companion, a youth who seemed about twenty-five, looked Sanjay in the eye, but also said nothing.

"It is no use talking to them," Collins told Sanjay in a matter-of-fact voice. "They are simpletons."

The weeping inside the tent halted briefly and the curtain parted. A woman looked out. Something about her broke Sanjay's heart. She was a tiny woman, barely five feet tall, dressed in a ragged sari. Her grainy complexion was streaked with tears.

Grief had ravaged her features – she seemed very old. She reminded Sanjay of his own mother. There was something universal about motherhood, he thought, and made a mental note to include the idea in his story.

"We're journalists," he repeated. "We want to interview you about your son."

She drew the end of her sari over her head.

"Who?" She looked at the men sitting outside for guidance.

"From Mumbai," said Collins with authority. The words sounded grand and the woman offered no resistance as he pushed his way past her into the shack. Sanjay was grateful to the photographer. He certainly had a way with these simple villagers.

It was surprisingly cool inside. Two small children were playing near a kerosene stove. There was a pallet on the floor. Next to it stood a small photograph of a man in orange garb with a halo around his head. His hand was raised in a gesture of benediction.

"Kamalabehn, when was the last time you saw your son?" Sanjay asked in a loud, clear voice.

She sat down on the floor and began to cry. Sanjay wanted to comfort her but had no idea how to begin. Collins came to the rescue again.

"We need more light," he said, looking around. "We have to go outside."

"We have to go outside," Sanjay repeated to the woman

in his loud voice. She rocked back and forth. There was something stagy about her grief, Sanjay thought. She looked exactly like a mother whose son had died. He liked the idea, but decided it wasn't something that would fit in an article about a martyr. He would use it some other time.

Collins put one hand on the woman's shoulder and pointed the way to the curtain with the cigarette he held in the other. She obediently rose and went outside. The two men sitting outside hadn't moved. She sat cross-legged on the ground. Collins went to the taxi to fetch his suitcase. Sanjay edged up beside the weeping mother.

"It's a good picture of your son," he said, indicating the framed photograph and lowering himself onto his haunches. "He was handsome."

She looked at Sanjay as if he was speaking gibberish. His neck burned in embarrassment. He ploughed on:

"Were you the one who instilled the love for the motherland in him?"

"God's will," she said, wiping her eyes with the end of her sari. "I told him not to go. He wouldn't listen."

"He died for the country," Sanjay countered. "For India, Bharat."

"Everything he wanted was here."

"All of India loves him. He was a great man. A patriot."

Collins came back with the flag and the tripod. He draped the cloth in the background over the edge of the shack and then moved the chair with the photo so that he could fit flag, mother and son in a single frame. The squatting youth watched the proceedings non-committally. His older companion stared at the ground. Sanjay shifted his weight. He was not used to sitting on his haunches and his toes were starting to ache.

"Was he the first person in the family to join the armed forces?"

"His grandfather lived here," she said distantly. "His father lived here. What was wrong with this village?"

"So his father was not in the army?" Sanjay said, hoping to lead the conversation to patriotic matters.

"You're going to publish the picture?" the youth asked abruptly.

"Yes," Sanjay said, feeling as if he had been found out. "We work for a newspaper. We're from Mumbai," he added, but failed to muster Collins' authority with the words.

"How much are you going to pay for it?"

"This is for India," Collins said, squinting through his camera. "For the nation's work, there is no question of payment."

"Once it is published in the paper, lots of money will come," Sanjay said. "People will read the article and want to compensate you for your loss."

Collins clicked his camera several times. A slight breeze picked up one end of the flag and caused it to flutter weakly. Collins clicked several times more.

"Nice shot," he said to himself.

He moved the tripod to a new angle. He peered through the camera again.

"Put your hand on the chair," he commanded the mother.

"Your hand," Sanjay repeated loudly in the woman's ear. "Put your hand on the chair."

She obeyed, placing a callused hand beside her son's photograph. Collins resumed clicking.

"How much money will they give?" the youth persisted.

"That depends on people's kindness," Sanjay replied. "Kamalabehn," he continued, "did your son write to you before he was killed?"

She seemed to collect her thoughts. "Why do you call me Kamalabehn?" she asked.

"I thought that was your name."

She shook her head.

"Her name is Mirabehn," the youth said.

"But this is your son, isn't it?" Sanjay indicated the picture.

"Of course."

"The ministry must have made a mistake."

"What ministry?"

"The Defence Ministry, of course. They are very proud of him."

The youth looked at Mirabehn.

"Why is the Defence Ministry proud of Gopal?"

"Gopal?" Sanjay exclaimed. "We thought his name was Pranlal."

"Pranlal's house is over there," the youth said, waving in the direction of the other shacks.

Sanjay pointed at the garlanded photograph on the chair. "But he's dead, too, isn't he?"

"He died in a train crash near Surat last week," the youth replied. "A signalman made a mistake."

Sanjay slowly pivoted and looked at Collins. The photographer stopped his clicking and lifted his head above the camera. His face was expressionless. He extracted the cigarette from his lips and contemplatively blew smoke.

The youth spoke: "How much money have they given in the past?"

"Who?" asked Sanjay laboriously. "Who gave money?"

"Your readers. How much do they usually give?"

Sanjay sighed. He wished he had a cigarette. A nice long drag was just what he needed.

The older man sitting beside the youth spoke for the first time. He told the youth, "Didn't you hear the young master? How much they give depends on people's kindness." He turned to Sanjay. "Isn't that so, sir?"

Sanjay nodded dully. "People's kindness. Yes, it all depends."

Collins dismantled the tripod. He strode past the grieving family and pulled his flag off the edge of the shack. The breeze lifted again and the cloth billowed into a bright, gay sail. The photographer battled to fold it. To Sanjay, he looked like an awkward sailor stranded outside his element, on the land.

Collins marched off towards the other shacks, muttering to himself. Sanjay smiled awkwardly at the mourning family. The grieving mother still had one hand resting on the chair.

"Is it all right," she asked, "if I go inside now?"

Rain

It was through a footnote in a scientific journal that Varun Dev learned about the Pakistani experiment to steal India's monsoon. The Indian meteorologist at the weather station in Amritsar squinted at the annotation: "See M. Ali's monograph about successful cloud-seeding experiments in Pakistan."

Mushtaq Ali was a meteorologist across the border in Lahore. He was about the same age as Varun Dev. Accordingly, the Indian scientist's first reaction had nothing to do with patriotism, pride or national security. He felt a twinge of jealousy that the Pakistani had been cited in the prestigious *Journal of Meteorology*. He noted with satisfaction that the footnote did not offer many details. Only a handful of meteorologists in the world would know who M. Ali was, and all worked near Amritsar and Lahore. No one who mattered would notice, certainly no one in America or England, which was where the journal was published.

To further console himself, Varun Dev read aloud from an invitation he had received to an important conference in London later that month. He injected a British accent in the interest of verisimilitude. He conjured up the plush conference centre, the give and take of repartee, the rapier thrusts of scientific conversation. The paper he planned to deliver about climate change in the Deccan Plateau was ready. In the small, shabby office that was his domain, he stood at an imaginary podium and delivered his speech, complete with gestures, knitted brows and interruptions for applause. As he left his office that evening, he convinced himself that Mushtaq Ali's citation was insignificant compared to his own impending triumph in London.

*   *   *   *   *

Varun Dev's triumph in London was diminished by the fact that Mushtaq Ali's monograph was on display at the conference. Even worse, the Pakistani scientist was at the conference, too, and the centre of attention of a large crowd of meteorologists who bombarded him with questions. Varun Dev noted bitterly that many of the questioners had British and American accents. The Indian smarted. His own presentation, an actual speech listed in the conference brochure, had been attended by only five people, two of whom stood near the door throughout the talk.

Varun Dev wiped the beads of perspiration that had gathered at his hairline. As he strolled past Mushtaq Ali's poster, he absent-mindedly glanced at the scientific equations to indicate they held only passing interest. But the moment he saw the headline of the newspaper article that was stuck alongside the scientific notations, he was transfixed. The article from *The Lahore Sentinel* was titled: "Drought in India versus Bumper Harvest in Pakistan: Local scientist draws rain clouds across the border."

"Varun, hello!" cried Mushtaq Ali through his crowd of admirers.

"Mushtaq–how are you?" Varun Dev could not suppress the iciness in his voice.

The Pakistani was unabashed: "I'm sorry I missed your presentation."

Varun Dev shrugged. "It's all right. Half the audience was standing."

Mushtaq Ali gestured helplessly at the throng around him. "I know what you mean."

The Pakistani scientist returned to the barrage of questions from his listeners. "It combines the old with the new," he told one questioner. "Everything we needed to know to seed clouds and draw rain was known already. The only confusion was the order of the procedure. That's why all previous attempts failed where we succeeded."

"What exactly is the procedure?" asked a scientist with an American accent.

"I cannot divulge," said Mushtaq Ali. "You see, that goes beyond scientific interest. That is now a matter of national security in Pakistan."

"But this is a conference of scientists," the American exclaimed. "There are no secrets between us."

"On the contrary, there are several secrets between us. The only difference is a scientist from the Third World now holds the most important secret of all."

Varun Dev marvelled that someone with skin as brown as his own could speak with such brashness.

"How do we know this really works?" asked another meteorologist.

"You'll have to take my word for it. You could also visit the Makran desert in Baluchistan where we have produced torrential rainfall." Mushtaq Ali glanced slyly at Varun Dev. "You could also ask my colleague here about the drought in north-western India last year. It is traditionally the most fertile area. But without rain, India will have to import grain next year. Maybe even from Pakistan. I have tasted rice from our paddy fields in the Makran desert. The flavour is unmatched."

Mushtaq Ali's grin was very wide. One of the western scientists turned to Varun Dev and asked, "is this true?"

The Indian meteorologist laughed dismissively. "What a question!" he exclaimed. "You're a group of scientists. You know that one year's rainfall means nothing. Yes, some areas of Punjab received less than usual rain, but what does that prove? We have no evidence yet of a pattern, and certainly no evidence that they —" Varun Dev bobbed his head at Mushtaq Ali — "were taking it away from us. If you ask me, the idea's absurd. Whoever heard of scientists presenting newspaper articles at a conference?"

And with that, Varun Dev swivelled and walked away. He raced to his hotel and barricaded himself in his suite. But there was no escape from the Pakistani scientist. He was the lead story on the television news that night and the focus of a talk show that followed. As Mushtaq Ali's claims grew progressively more expansive, Varun Dev ordered a bottle of scotch and methodically got drunk. At midnight, Mushtaq Ali was still talking for the umpteenth time about the stupid rain in his stupid desert, and when the television station aired a photograph of Pakistani bedouins tramping knee deep through waterlogged rice fields, Varun Dev was no longer sure whether the apparition was a figment of Mushtaq Ali's junk science or the effect of the scotch on his brain.

When the telephone rang at two in the morning, Varun Dev was in a state unfit for intelligent conversation. He was fast asleep, sprawled half in and half out of the couch. The scene before him looked like a carefully contrived movie set. The lights were on. Shards of glass lay scattered over the coffee table and the floor – at some point, the bottle of scotch had been smashed. The television was blaring, although by now the soggy bedouins had been replaced by a cast of skittish Englishwomen who were running around in their underwear and squeaking in Cockney accents about a lost dog.

Varun Dev regarded the scene. Through the fog of scotch, it made no sense. The ringing telephone appeared to be part of the hallucination. He waited for it to go away, but it continued to ring. He reluctantly answered the phone, like a man forced to participate in a magic trick.

"H-hyes?"

"Is this Varun Dev?"

The Indian meteorologist cautiously conceded the fact. The voice at the other end of the line was brusque.

"This is Ranjit Malhotra. I'm with the Indian High Commissioner's office in London."

Varun Dev sniggered. One of the women in the television show had bent over a bush and toppled into it. Her bare legs kicked in the air.

"Are you watching the show, too?" Varun Dev asked in a friendly voice.

"What show?"

"I don't know," the Indian meteorologist said apologetically. "Whatever is on."

"Goddammit Dev, pull yourself together. Did you hear what I said? I'm with the Indian High Commissioner's office in —"

"Lon-Don. Yes, yes, you told me that," said Varun Dev with some asperity. "Tell me," he continued, as the leggy Englishwoman on TV was extricated by the other leggy Englishwomen, "do you find blonde women attractive?"

When there was no response, he volunteered his own opinion. "I think it depends. On the blonde woman, I mean. Some blonde women are attractive while others are not. Take this woman, for instance. I'd say that—"

"Dev!" roared Ranjit Malhotra. "You're drunk and incompetent. If you don't pull yourself together, I'm going to get you fired."

The Indian meteorologist slowly considered the possibility that the voice on the phone was real and that his career might actually be at stake. He pulled himself upright, clicked off the television and swallowed. He shook his head to clear it.

"I'm sorry, sir, I was asleep when you called—"

"Enough of that," replied Ranjit Malhotra shortly. "I've been trying to reach you for hours. The damn fools at the weather conference didn't know which hotel you were staying at. Have you heard about the breach of our national security?"

Varun Dev racked his brains, but all he could recall was Mushtaq Ali's rain-seeding experiments. "No, sir."

"You mean to tell me the Government of India paid all this money to send you to this damn conference and you missed the biggest story under your nose?"

Varun Dev coughed to give himself time to think.

"Were you even at the damn conference?" bellowed Ranjit Malhotra. His voice, now that he had warmed up, easily hit a booming baritone. "Have you been drunk in your room the last three days?

"No sir, I was at the conference. My presentation was standing room only–"

"Surely you must have heard about this Mushtaq Ali?"

"Mushtaq? Mushtaq Ali?" The Indian meteorologist felt a weight lift from his shoulders. "Yes, I know all about Mushtaq. He's actually a good friend of mine. He has come up with this hare-brained scheme to produce rain in the desert. Can you imagine – camels ploughing paddy fields in Baluchistan? Hahahaha –" Varun Dev broke off because he remembered that Ranjit Malhotra had said that there had been a breach of national security. Now he was confused again. He tried to focus. He wished he had not drunk so much scotch. He cautiously ventured, "The breach of national security. Did you mean – the rain?"

"It is clear to me that this means nothing to you, Dev, but thousands of people in Punjab have suffered because your friend has stolen our monsoon. Their livelihoods have been destroyed and there is talk of famine. The Prime Minister has summoned me to New Delhi and I am leaving in two hours. Now listen carefully. You have the option of joining me at Heathrow and helping your country deal with this catastrophe. Or you can sit in your hotel room and get drunk and talk nonsense about your Pakistani friends. If you choose the second, you should think twice about setting foot in India again."

Ranjit Malhotra hung up. It took Varun Dev about five seconds to make up his mind. Then, because he was young, smart and agile, even if he had drunk too much scotch, he leaped up and began packing. On the way to the airport, as his cab bumped its way along the silent streets of London, the Indian meteorologist began composing a memo. He wrote, "A Report on the Pakistani attempt to destabilise India by stealing the subcontinent's most precious natural resource." He underlined the title twice. As he began to write, he noticed that it was raining outside.

A short while later, Varun Dev was ushered onto the Air India plane. His face was flushed, because of the continued effects of the scotch and because he was embarrassed by his dismal phone performance. It could ruin his career and make him a laughingstock in the scientific community. In the first class cabin, Ranjit Malhotra was instantly recognisable. He had the physique of a weightlifter. Streaks of silver ran through his hair, giving him an air of dignified authority. He glanced up from the papers spread before him.

"Good morning, sir," Varun Dev said, trying hard not to bow. "I'm really very sorry–"

"Dev, let us see if we understand each another," growled the older man, stroking his luxuriant moustache. "Do you know what this damn Mushtaq Ali has done? Scientifically, are you on top of what's going on?"

"Ah – of course, sir," Varun Dev said. "It's all basic meteorological stuff. Elementary, really."

"Have you taken notes at the conference?"

"Extensive notes."

"We can replicate what they have done?"

"We can do even better. I have begun composing a memo about the details of the Pakistani plan."

"Good man." Ranjit Malhotra clapped the Indian scientist on the shoulder.

"About the things I said earlier tonight, sir–"

"Forget about it. It's going to stay between us. You are the man of the hour and nothing else matters."

"Yes, sir."

As the plane took off, Ranjit Malhotra attended to a stream of telephone calls from top officials in New Delhi. Mushtaq Ali's news from the London conference had been broadcast on morning TV shows in India and caused an instant uproar. Politicians from Opposition parties immediately began to grandstand about the ill-prepared state of the country's security under the current regime. Interspersed with footage of barren fields in Punjab came calls for the Prime Minister's resignation.

"Why do we have to hear about this breach of our national security from the BBC?" asked one Opposition leader. "Why were Indian meteorologists not alert? What was Indian Intelligence doing?"

Footage was shown of farmers bemoaning the strange

drought that had befallen them and ruined their livelihood. It was difficult enough to eke out a life in agriculture, said the leader of one farmer's group, without worrying that a foreign power was stealing your rain. Some political parties called for outright war. "We want our rain back," said one leader. "If they won't return it, we should march in and take it."

A spokesman at the Pakistani High Commission in Delhi pointed out that with nuclear weapons in the subcontinent, any unprovoked aggression would meet with catastrophic consequences.

On the hotline from the airplane, Ranjit Malhotra assured his frantic counterparts in Delhi that a talented Indian scientist at the London Conference had collected detailed information about the Pakistani experiment and was ready to replicate it in India. The government quickly trumpeted the fact on national television. As soon as the plane landed in Delhi, Ranjit Malhotra and Varun Dev were mobbed by reporters.

"If Pakistan does not back down, we have the scientific capacity to permanently draw away all their rain," declared Ranjit Malhotra. "Our scientists are several generations ahead of theirs. We can not only return the Makran desert in Baluchistan to the camels and the cacti, we can turn all of Pakistan into a desert."

They walked out of the airport to a waiting limousine. The television cameras, with their tripods and cables, followed like spiders after prey. The limousine sped away to the Prime Minister's office. Two police jeeps escorted them through the streets of Delhi with sirens blaring. Constables stationed at key intersections saluted stiffly as the convoy passed. Through the limousine's tinted windows, Varun Dev saw columns of stalled motorists. Wide-eyed pedestrians whispered among each other, trying to identify the dignitaries who were the cause of such commotion. In what seemed like a matter of minutes, Varun Dev and Ranjit Malhotra were whisked past commandos guarding the Prime Minister's conference room. The Indian scientist reflected that the turn of events bore a curious similarity to the drunken hallucinations that had started the previous night. Here he was, visiting the Prime Minister of India and being saluted by men wielding automatic weapons, when a few hours before he had watched bedouins tramp through water-logged deserts and leggy Englishwomen fall into bushes. His temples throbbed with a hangover. But there was no time to dwell on it. The Prime Minister, with the rest of the cabinet in the background, welcomed him and Ranjit Malhotra and shook their hands and told them that they were the lynchpins of the country's national security.

In his introductory remarks, after everyone sat around a large table, Ranjit Malhotra explained how an Indian scientist had come to monitor the Pakistani experiment. "We had been concerned about the activities of Pakistani meteorologists for a long time," he said. "Well before Dr. Varun Dev was assigned to monitor the London Conference, he had been closely tracking the activities of Mushtaq Ali. Dr. Dev was chosen for this sensitive mission because he was at the nearest Indian weather station to Ali's activities in Lahore, and because he himself was involved in rain-seeding experiments of an advanced stage. Obviously, in the interest of national security, all of this was kept top secret. Even Dr. Dev's colleagues in Amritsar had no idea. In London, Dr. Dev and I worked closely at all times and I am pleased to report that we now possess all the Pakistani plans. As directed by the Prime Minister, we can turn Pakistan into a desert."

There were appreciative murmurs around the table. Varun Dev felt a savage thirst and drained his glass of water. Ranjit Malhotra had just conferred a doctorate on him. It was something they had agreed upon, but this was the first time he heard the word "doctor" appended to his name. It gave him a strange, otherworldly feeling, as if the old Varun Dev had died and, in his place, like a caterpillar moulting into a butterfly, had emerged the sleek and distinguished Dr. Dev. An orderly refilled his water glass. The Prime Minister leaned forward with a question.

"Dr. Dev, when did you first hear about the Pakistani plans?"

"The Pakistanis have been trying rain-seeding experiments for several years, sir. I obtained detailed plans of the current experiment about a month ago."

"And you immediately realised its importance?"

"Absolutely, sir. As Mr. Malhotra explained, the primary focus of my visit to the meteorological conference in London was to monitor Mushtaq Ali's activities."

"India is grateful for your alertness," the Prime Minister said. "When this is over, the nation will properly demonstrate its gratitude."

"The honour and security of the nation is all the reward any citizen can seek, sir," Varun Dev said humbly.

The discussion around the table veered to the rain that Pakistan had already stolen and whether a demand ought to be lodged for its return.

"The rain would have soaked into the ground by now," pointed out the Irrigation Minister. "It will be difficult to retrieve."

"It would also have been soaked up by the grains that were grown," pointed out the Agriculture Minister. "Perhaps we should ask for the return of the rain in the form of grain."

"Rain or grain, that's the question," assented the Prime Minister, who liked wordplay.

"A lot of it would have been eaten by rats because Pakistan has terrible granaries," said the Minister for Health, who disliked the Agriculture Minister and enjoyed sniping at him. "Should we ask for the rats, too?"

Varun Dev marvelled. He had no idea that Cabinet meetings went like this.

The Minister for Science, Space and Technology said, "Our satellite imagery can show which parts of the desert have become the most fertile and –"

The Defence Minister thumped the table and all the glasses of water slid sideways by an inch.

"We can't get any of it back and we know it," he said. "The Pakistanis will laugh if we ask for either the rain or the grain. They will say the clouds crossed the border and dropped the rain in Baluchistan. The rain doesn't come stamped, "made in India." We will look like idiots on the world stage if we make stupid demands."

"But if we don't do something, we will lose a no-confidence motion in Parliament," said the Agriculture Minister.

"And the next election, too. This year, the Pakistanis stole rain from Punjab. Next year, they could divert the monsoon right before it hits south India and make it go to Pakistan. Maybe even Kuwait and Iran. The whole of the Middle East could become fertile. They could be growing mangoes and watermelons in Saudi Arabia next year. Where will it end?"

The Prime Minister abjectly turned to Varun Dev: "Can that happen?"

"Of course not!" the Indian scientist blurted with a laugh that he quickly suppressed. "I mean, not if we do something about it."

"But what can we do?"

"Sir, if I may interject," said Ranjit Malhotra smoothly, extricating from his briefcase the memo that Varun Dev had composed. "We have a plan to halt the Pakistanis. But it will need resources. I recommend we set up an emergency office under your supervision."

There were nods of agreement around the table.

"Let us do it immediately," the Prime Minister said. "Tell us what you need. Our goal is to recover the monsoon."

The meeting broke up. The Prime Minister shook Varun Dev's hand. "Dr. Dev, the nation is depending on you."

"I'll do my best, sir," said the Indian meteorologist. "God-willing, we will bring back the rain."

The following day, Varun Dev found himself installed at the new Centre for the Development of Rain in India. He spun his brand new leather chair from the magnificent view through the windows to the row of sleek telephones on his teakwood desk. The telephones were black, green, white and red, and the meteorologist picked them up one by one to ascertain whether they all had dial tones. All did, except the last, which produced a well-modulated voice that had learned its accent at one of Delhi's elite ladies' colleges.

"Yes, sir?"

"Is this a cross-connection?" asked Varun Dev.

"No, this is Priya, your secretary."

"Ah. Priya, how are you?"

"I'm fine, sir. Is there anything you want?"

Varun Dev raced through his mind for anything he might want from Priya Bhalla.

"I was just making sure the telephone worked," he finally said.

"Is there anything else, sir?"

"No, thank you."

He hung up and grimaced at not having come up with a casual, yet humorous, remark. He felt so inexperienced with women. To release his frustration, he spun his chair round and round. Faster and faster he went until his head and the room were spinning and then there was a perfunctory knock on the door and Ranjit Malhotra entered. Varun Dev skidded the chair to a halt and tried to look his boss in the eye, but he appeared to be travelling sideways.

"Let's get to work," said Ranjit Malhotra.

"Right," said the meteorologist, reaching for the edge of the desk to give himself a sense of stability.

"Why are you swaying like that? Have you been drinking again?"

"Of course not."

"Look Dev, no more funny business from you. This is a most sensitive mission."

"Most sensitive," the meteorologist said with a wink. "We sit in our offices and wait for the monsoon rains next year. I think we can manage to do that."

Ranjit Malhotra sized up the scientist. "You have been drinking again, I see. There's no other way I can explain this careless attitude. It is costing the treasury hundreds of thousands of rupees to maintain these offices and hire a small army of staff. If we don't show results, they will vanish like that." Ranjit Malhotra snapped his fingers. "Do I make myself clear?"

"Yes, sir."

"I expect detailed plans from you before the end of the day. I have told the Prime Minister that I shall provide him with weekly updates. Action, that's what we need. Immediate and forceful action."

"I shall draw up the plans immediately," said the meteorologist.

Ranjit Malhotra spun and left the room, shutting the door with a thud.

The meteorologist stared at the closed door. Ranjit

Malhotra did not want to know the truth: The Pakistani experiment consisted of nothing more than a freak diversion of the monsoon and an opportunistic scientist in Lahore. Strange weather was to be expected occasionally – science predicted that there would be such anomalies. There was nothing to indicate that anyone knew how to make the rain change course. Much as he liked his new office and the array of telephones and the hotline to Priya Bhalla's modulated voice, Varun Dev felt lonely. He stared at the row of weather-related books and journals on his desk. Finally he sighed and summoned Priya Bhalla into the room to take a memo.

She sat across the desk from him, notebook ready. She had almond-shaped eyes and Varun Dev spun his chair around to face the window so he wouldn't be distracted. He could see the faint outline of her reflection in the glass. She was looking back at him, too, and he remembered that brides and grooms in traditional marriages first glimpsed each other through their reflections in a mirror before the veil between them was drawn away.

"Here are the supplies I will need," he said, trying to keep his voice level. "Four weather balloons a day, each equipped with temperature, humidity and wind pattern gauges. Factory level production of silver iodide and dry ice. I will need a plane capable of spraying 500 hectares a day and eight to ten towers with built-in flares. Also a helicopter for reconnaissance missions—make that two helicopters—and trained pilots capable of flying in all weather conditions."

Maybe it would work. Maybe it would produce the torrential rainfall that the Prime Minister and the cabinet wanted, maybe it would lead to re-election campaigns for the politicians and promotions for Ranjit Malhotra and medals of honour from a grateful nation. When it came to the weather, who knew what would happen?

The next week, Varun Dev asked Priya Bhalla to accompany him on a helicopter reconnaissance flight over the parched fields of Punjab. He hardly slept the night before the trip, knowing that this would be their first time together in such a confined space. He imagined himself masterfully directing her attention to various landmarks and meteorological conditions. He thought about suitable openings for small talk and banter. He imagined she was fearful of heights, and saw himself gently reassuring her. He finally got out of bed at five in the morning, shaved twice, and slathered on deodorant and after-shave lotion. He expected she would show up in a sari, but instead she wore workmanlike trousers and a shirt with an open collar. It still made Varun Dev think of all things lush and beautiful – apples, pomegranates and mangoes.

"Did you sleep well?" he asked.

"Yes." She looked surprised at the question.

Varun Dev reminded himself that there was no reason why Priya Bhalla would not have slept well. He chivalrously offered her a hand to climb into the helicopter, but she sprang up easily on her own.

"Did you have a restful night?" she asked politely, after he struggled into place beside her.

"No," he confessed. He blushed and quickly added, "I was doing complex meteorological calculations to estimate how we could bring back the monsoon."

She smiled at him and he felt like the smartest man in the world.

"Are we ready, sir?" the pilot asked.

"Yes, yes, why not?" Varun Dev said, settling back into his seat.

Priya Bhalla coughed and gestured. Varun Dev did not understand. She pointedly glanced down.

"What is it?" he said, flustered.

He followed her gaze down to his lap and a surge of mortification swept over him. Was his zip undone? He checked the zip and she giggled.

"Your seatbelt, sir," she said.

"Yes, of course."

He was sitting on the buckle and she had to help extricate it from under him. The engine revved. With what he hoped was an expression of suave nonchalance, he turned to her.

"You know —" he began genially, and then his mind went totally blank. He could not remember a single topic he had meant to discuss with her. It was she who came to the rescue.

"What's the basic concept in retrieving the rain?" she asked as the helicopter took off.

It was an elementary and obvious question, and Varun Dev realised that it was the first time anyone had asked it. Not the Prime Minister or the Cabinet, and certainly not Ranjit Malhotra had thought to ask him what exactly was involved.

"It's difficult to explain to lay people," Varun Dev said, assuming what he hoped was a thoughtful expression. "There are so many factors involved. Wind, moisture, temperature. That's why they say dealing with the weather is an art as much as a science."

"I'd like to learn as we go along, if you'll teach me," she said.

"I don't see why not. It will be my pleasure."

The passenger seats were close together and their knees brushed against each other. The side of his thigh closest to her was sharply attuned to the slightest contact. He did not want to give the pilot the wrong impression and therefore leaned chastely away – the armrest they shared went unused.

"I hope you are not bothered by heights – you don't have vertigo?" he asked.

She informed him that her father had been a fighter pilot and that she had been flying in planes and helicopters since she was three.

"Good, good," Varun Dev said genially, striking that issue off his list of topics.

It was a cloudless day, essentially useless for meteorology, but perfect for a joyride. Beneath them, the landscape unfurled like a giant quilt, a patchwork of fields. Where the quilt was usually a multitude of greens, it was now a canvas of varying shades of brown.

"God blessed Punjab with fertile soil and ample rain," he said, indicating the dry, caked fields. "There is no other explanation for such ideal conditions for agriculture. Who are we to protest if this bounty is withheld for one year?"

"But it's the Pakistanis who have stolen the rain!"

"Does anyone know how to steal the rain?" he asked gently. "How do we know the Pakistanis have stolen the rain?"

"You said so yourself in your report to the Cabinet!"

"Yes - yes, of course," he said hastily. He smiled to imply that she had passed his test. "The Pakistanis have stolen the rain."

"And you are going to bring it back," she said righteously. "Aren't you – Varun?"

Varun Dev's heart raced. He could not refuse her. Even if what she wanted was a reconfiguration of the laws of physics. "Yes," he said. "I will. That is, we will. You and I, together."

She smiled and squared her shoulders against the challenges ahead, and the meteorologist noticed that her breasts strained boldly against her shirt. His scientific misgivings drowned as patriotism and pride swirled in a potent whirlpool with tenderness and lust. Priya Bhalla was Punjab and Punjab was India and he would love his country as he loved her and together they would retrieve the rain and restore the land to fecundity. Over the next days, they began spraying the clouds.

With each request he made for supplies, Varun Dev felt certain that he would be turned down, that some government scientist would ask him why he needed tons of solvents and drumfuls of silver iodide. It turned out to be exactly the opposite. The more expensive his work became, the more elaborate his plans, the better the nation seemed to feel and the more warmly were his requisitions received at the Prime Minister's office. Word about his effort spread to the media and on a couple of occasions, Varun Dev allowed reporters to fly with him on reconnaissance missions. He took care to remain tight-lipped and withdrawn. The profiles in the newspapers painted a picture of an iconoclast and a recluse – essential ingredients of the brilliant scientist.

More and more planes were pressed into his service, gathering information, flying sorties, and spraying clouds with exotic potions. His staff expanded to fill two whole floors of prime Delhi real estate. Varun Dev grew used to striding into military rooms of the Indian Air Force and nodding grimly at stiff salutes. He took to wearing military fatigues as he directed the missions. Like the World War II photographs he had seen of Winston Churchill and General Patton, he would place one boot on a chair as he stood before a table peering at large maps. He would then solemnly stick his index finger at the targets he wanted hit that day.

As the project expanded, Varun Dev launched dozens of imported weather balloons. Television bulletins said anyone who found a balloon should return it to the nearest operations centre. Although each balloon could have been dismantled and sold for an astronomical price on the black market, the farmers and peasants of Punjab rallied behind the meteorological effort. Corruption took a backseat to patriotism, and the balloons were retrieved with fervour.

Only one scientist raised doubts. A fellow called Lakshman Murthy from the Indian Institute of Science in Bangalore demanded that Varun Dev reveal the list of solvents he was spraying, and suggested that the public health could be endangered by spraying tons of chemicals into the atmosphere. Varun Dev obtained a copy of the Bangalore Times, where the interview was published on the front page, and spent a weekend in a fever of panic. He imagined the headlines that would follow: "Varun Dev a Quack" and "India Fails to Cajole Monsoon." The plush offices would disappear, and his career would be finished. Varun Dev realised the thing he feared most was Priya Bhalla's scorn.

He finally telephoned Ranjit Malhotra and read out excerpts from the interview. "What are we going to do?" he pleaded.

"Do? We're going ahead!" bellowed Ranjit Malhotra. "Who the hell is this damn Murthy?"

Newspapers the following week carried articles saying the Bangalore meteorologist had been found guilty of scientific misconduct, and that he had been suspended. Ranjit Malhotra spent an hour explaining to Varun Dev that unpatriotic curmudgeons would always criticise others out of professional jealousy. All right-thinking Indians knew Varun Dev's grand scheme was built on the strongest scientific foundations.

The lowest point of the operation turned out to be its pinnacle. Four months into the massive military and civilian effort, two planes collided during a tricky cloud-spraying mission. Both pilots were instantly killed. There was a national outpouring of sorrow and flags were flown at half-mast. The air force organised a mammoth memorial service that was attended by the entire central cabinet. Varun Dev stood next to the Prime Minister in a dark suit as the ceremonial guns boomed. Rather than having to apologise for his ill-conceived scheme, Varun Dev found himself sombrely shaking hands with senior military brass and exchanging condolences.

The Prime Minister made a stirring speech about how the death would not deter the Indians from completing their mission. "Take heart," he told an ashen-faced Varun Dev. "This is like war and there will be casualties in war. It is only a reminder that we must fight harder."

The moment was captured on national television. The disaster added credibility and resources to Varun Dev's operations. To question him now would be to question the deaths of the pilots, who had become martyrs.

Priya Bhalla framed a photograph of the Prime Minister shaking Varun Dev's hand and placed it prominently on her desk. The meteorologist felt better about himself than he ever had, more in charge of his destiny. He was increasingly open about his feelings for Priya Bhalla and discovered that his self-confidence was met receptively by her.

As summer approached and the time for the monsoon rains arrived, anxious messengers arrived from the Prime Minister's office asking Varun Dev about the likelihood of the operation's success. Varun Dev was unruffled: He had come to realise that he could not lose. Hundreds of people had been pressed into his service and an incalculable amount of money had been spent. Men had even died implementing his plans. In the end, people would not really care whether he was right or wrong – when it came to matters of national pride, what they really wanted was a pageant of patriotism. More than rain, they wanted heroism and drama, and he had provided them with extraordinary theatre.

The monsoon arrived exactly on schedule. The torrential downpours were greeted with the usual celebrations, except that this year everyone agreed that each drop that fell was solely because of a reclusive scientist named Varun Dev. He was feted in villages across Punjab. Men and women prostrated themselves before him. The Prime Minister's office constantly requested his presence at official ceremonies in advance of the coming general elections.

In late August, Varun Dev, Priya Bhalla and Ranjit Malhotra slipped out of a banquet hall where they had been honoured yet again. The meteorologist's head spun – numerous glasses of alcohol had been thrust into his hands. As they stepped outside, he placed one arm around Priya Bhalla's waist and the other around Ranjit Malhotra's shoulders.

He felt very much in love, very lucky and very drunk. The combination usually spurs men to speak the truth: "Amazing, isn't it, what people will believe?" he said.

"What do you mean?" asked Ranjit Malhotra.

"The rain," said Varun Dev. "As if anybody knows how to control the rain."

Ranjit Malhotra exchanged glances with Priya Bhalla.

"You're going to have to look after him," he told her. "He could have a great future, but he's got to stop blabbering after he's had a drink."

"I'll look after him," she replied, drawing Varun Dev's arm tighter around her waist. She was an experienced intelligence agent, and Ranjit Malhotra knew she would keep her word.

Sakina

It was not yet four o'clock when she rolled off the mattress and felt in the dark for her slippers. The floor was icy cold and her toes curled in on themselves. She sighed. A plume of breath sprang from her lips. Like a smoker, she thought. Seeing that her parents were still asleep on the other mattress, she placed two fingers at her lips and inhaled, then let out a long burst of 'smoke.' She sucked again on her fingers and pretended to stumble drunkenly to the bathroom like the vamps in movies. She dipped a mug into a bucket of water, poured the water into a cupped hand and splashed it on her face. The cold made her gasp and brought her fully awake. She rinsed her mouth. The chill of the water made her teeth hurt. She went to the kitchen and set the kettle to boil. She heard her parents shift in their sleep. But neither arose and Sakina knew that they would not wake up until she had brought them their tea.

"Father, get up, it's late," she said, placing the steaming cup and saucer beside him.

"Mother, another late start today."

She said these things to them every day, whether it was early on a weekday or late on Sundays, which meant five-thirty. Sakina had recently assumed the role of preparing the morning tea from her mother. Like her role model, she assumed that offering some criticism while serving the tea was part of her duties. Like most complaints in the family, it meant nothing and would not be taken seriously. But in the long list of accusations and disagreements and scoldings they would exchange during the course of the day, this was her opening salvo.

Sakina returned to the kitchen where two cups of tea sat steaming. She drained one and gasped. Her breath felt like real smoke. She placed the fourth cup on a saucer, struck a match and lit a candle. Holding the candle in one hand and the saucer in the other, she made her way down a narrow set of steps to a cellar. A pile of rags was strewn on the floor and Sakina kicked them aside. A roughly cut wooden panel was revealed – it was a makeshift trapdoor. She set the candle down beside it and rapped on it with her knuckles.

"Hey you, down there, wake up. It's late!" she whispered.

Almost instantly, the trapdoor was pushed open. The man kept his face in the shadows but Sakina could see his eyes glinting at her in the candlelight.

"I was already up," he said in a thin, haughty voice.

She handed him his tea without further comment. In the week since he had arrived, Sakina had not worked out a suitable greeting. Each day, he contradicted whatever criticism she offered and reduced her to silence. She sat on her haunches, held her knees, and rocked back and forth. She tried to look bored. He sipped the tea, his features obscured by the sharp shadow of the trapdoor. She could only see the white teacup moving back and forth in the candlelight and being tipped into the darkness that was his mouth. He hid like this every day. She suspected he was watching her. She told herself she was too old for such childish games, even as she congratulated herself for occasionally catching a glimpse of his lips. They were sensuous, and glistened after each sip of tea.

He held out the empty cup and saucer to her without comment or thanks. She expected neither – such niceties only came from educated folk, whose gracious words usually concealed darker motives. She brushed his fingers as she took the cup and noted with surprise that they were warm. The cellar was freezing cold.

"I'll bring breakfast later on," Sakina told him, as she collected the candle and stood up.

"Don't forget to cover the trapdoor," he replied, pulling the wooden panel shut.

Sakina contemptuously kicked the rags into place. For a man who came up with an original answer to everything she said, he was boring and repetitive about this piece of advice. "Don't forget to cover the trapdoor," he said every day, as if she would forget such an important aspect of harbouring a fugitive. She climbed the steps to the living room and thought about a pithy line to throw at him the next day. Maybe she could say, "Of course I will, you fool," or better still, "cover it yourself." Ha, that would be a clever thing to say! It would serve him right. "Cover it yourself–"

She heard the low murmur of conversation as she reached the top of the stairs. She stopped and placed her ear at the door that opened into the living room.

"For the hundredth time, this madness must end," her mother was saying. "It's been a week and he was to have only stayed a night. What kind of environment is this for a child?"

"Jamilah, what is there to do?" replied her father, in his usual placatory tone. "It is the times we are going through."

"This is different. This is war. We should have left Kashmir long ago."

"Where would we go?"

"Some place where we can raise a child without worrying if we will be alive tomorrow."

"Sakina is old enough to understand."

"What are you talking about, Aftab? She is fourteen. What if someone hears something? The police can raid the house—"

"Jamilah, we've talked about this before. Tell me yourself, what is to be done?"

"Ask him to leave."

"I have asked him already. He says, soon, in another day or two. His plans have been delayed—"

"I do not believe it, I do not believe him. Aftab, this is not a game for little people. When the elephants fight, it is the grass that gets trampled. You must get him to leave. Insist on it."

"Jamilah, what is wrong with you? Mohsin brought him here. Did you remember how Mohsin behaved? If Mohsin Saeed himself is afraid of this man, how should we behave? We cannot insist on anything."

"No," Jamilah agreed slowly. "We cannot insist."

"We must tread carefully. Perhaps he will soon leave on his own and we can put this behind us."

"I'm very afraid."

"Yes," he said simply. "I am afraid, too. Sometimes it seems that Sakina is the only one who is not afraid."

"The child has not yet learned the meaning of fear."

Sakina rolled her eyes. She heard her father get up and go to the bathroom. She tiptoed down a few steps and then climbed back up noisily. She opened the door with a flourish and stepped into the living room.

"Since when did you go down there dressed like that?" Jamilah demanded.

"Dressed like what?" said Sakina saucily, blowing out the candle.

"Like that. Wearing next to nothing. Have you no modesty?"

"No." Sakina pouted her lips and was pleased at her repartee.

"I shall have to have a word with your father."

"Have a word. Have several words. What do I care?"

Sakina provocatively sashayed past her mother to the kitchen, although her hips were so slender that they did not produce the desired effect of lasciviousness. Her mother pulled a shawl tight around her head, as if increasing the display of her own modesty would compensate for her daughter's shamelessness.

They prepared the morning meal together. Sakina hummed a tune to indicate that her mother's criticism had not affected her. Jamilah recited under her breath a litany of chores that had to be completed that day. Sakina's father shuffled about the narrow living room. Their home was really just a large room that had been partitioned into a tiny bedroom, a living room, kitchen and bath. It was identical to hundreds of other homes in the poor neighbourhood. The cellar with the trapdoor was the only anomaly. The merchant who rented them the house had offered no explanations for it.

It was Mohsin Saeed who had directed them to the house. From her parents' deferential behaviour to him, Sakina guessed that Saeed was paying part of the rent and the expenses of starting a tailoring business. When Saeed told them he might need the cellar from time to time for storage, they had readily agreed – Aftab and Jamilah had not expected human cargo.

Sakina eyed her mother out of the corner of one eye. Jamilah was laboriously kneading a mound of dough. Flecks of grey hair fell over her prematurely wrinkled forehead. Sakina wished her parents could have been dashing and daring, instead of being perpetually afraid of their own shadows.

"How long is this man going to stay with us?" Sakina asked casually.

Jamilah stiffened.

"Why? What's wrong? Has he been talking to you?"

"Of course not," said Sakina exasperatedly. "Just the opposite, in fact. He hides in the shadows when I take him his food and he never says anything other than, 'don't forget to cover the trapdoor.' I just want to know how many more days I will have to bother with feeding him."

"He'll be gone soon. I don't want you to exchange even

one word with him. Sakina, do you understand? Children should be seen, not—"

"I'm not a child."

"You are as far as he is concerned. Understand? Not one word."

Sakina made a face and thought of the most inflammatory thing she could say.

"Why?" she asked. "Is he with the mujahideen? Has he come in from Pakistan?"

Jamilah uttered a little shriek and slapped her daughter across the face. Her palm left behind the imprint of a welter laced with dough. Then, as if she was the one who had been struck, Jamilah burst into tears. Sakina scowled. Hot, rebellious words welled up in her, but she held them back.

Aftab poked his head into the kitchen and saw the hostility on his daughter's face and the piteous expression on his wife's face. His eyes narrowed.

"I'm going downstairs," he said shortly. "I'll be back."

He lit a candle and shuffled down the steps to the cellar. Sakina heard the knock on the trapdoor and the greeting her father exchanged with the fugitive, but thereafter their conversation became impossible to hear. She strained to listen.

"Don't try to eavesdrop," said Jamilah, between sobs.

"I wasn't eavesdropping. What makes you think I was eavesdropping?" Sakina's eyes flashed indignantly.

Jamilah shook her head as tears ran down her cheeks.

"Curses befall the curious," she said.

When the meal was ready and the house somewhat warmer, Jamilah retired to the bathroom to bathe. Sakina nibbled distractedly at her food. Then, abruptly, she rose and filled two plates with food, put them on a tray and noiselessly tiptoed to the cellar.

"I cannot do it," she heard her father say, as she placed a cautious foot on the first step. "What if someone spots me as I am carrying it across town? It is too dangerous."

"Aftab Ahsan's family is already in danger because of my presence," the fugitive replied, using polite and indirect language. "If Aftab Ahsan performs this one favour for us, I will complete my mission and be able to leave his home."

"If it could be done, I would do it. But I have a family to think about. I am not a guerrilla."

Sakina crept down the stairs. She saw her father first. He was sitting on his haunches with his back to her and, as usual, his posture was bowed and respectful. A small cloth bag was on the floor beside him, and stains of what appeared to be grease showed through the cloth. Jagged edges protruded through the fabric. The fugitive was sitting cross-legged on the cellar floor. Sakina saw his face for the first time and the breath caught in her throat. He was a young man with a week-old beard that gave him a hungry look, like the photographs of models in magazines. In the candlelight, his eyes appeared jet-black. His eyebrows were fine and his jaw was sharp and square. It was a dangerous and handsome face, she decided. Her lips parted. The step creaked beneath her and the youth glanced up. Aftab Ahsan whirled.

"Who told you to come down here?" Sakina's father demanded.

"I was bringing the breakfast before it went cold—"

The youth moved a rag to cover the bundle. Sakina stared at it. The fugitive kept a hand on the bundle, as if it were a dog.

"Go upstairs at once," commanded her father. "I have told you not to come here while I am talking to our, our – guest."

"I'll leave the food."

Sakina left the tray on the ground. She glanced at the youth. He had turned his face away, but she could swear he was smiling.

"Close the door behind you," said her father shortly.

Sakina climbed the stairs. She felt self-conscious. It had been different before, when she had not been able to see the young man and only he had been able to see her. Now she knew what he looked like and the knowledge made her shy.

"Your daughter has been very kind to me," she heard the youth tell her father.

"She does not know when she should not intrude—"

"It does not matter," he said in a voice that was intended to carry. "You must be proud to have such a beautiful daughter."

Sakina's heart pounded. She did not hear her father's response but was sure he was angry with the young man for flirting so openly. A hot flush rose to her cheeks and she was suddenly aware of the shabby clothes she wore and her inadequate figure. She thought of all the times in the past week when she had taken food to the cellar without even combing her hair, let alone attending to some make-up or a pair of earrings. What must he have thought as he sipped his tea in the shadow of the cellar trapdoor? She bit her lip.

"Have you eaten?" asked Jamilah, as she emerged from the bathroom.

"No," Sakina said. "I'm not hungry."

Sakina waited for her father to emerge from the cellar before she went to take a bath. But she only pretended to bathe, swirling her hand through the bucket of water and hurling mugfuls at the wall. Between splashes, she placed her ear at the bathroom door. As she expected, Aftab was telling Jamilah about the fugitive's request.

"What is in the bag?" Jamilah asked.

"I don't know," said Aftab evasively. "It looked like newspapers."

"Newspapers?"

"That's what I said."

"I wonder how they got into the cellar. Did he bring them with him?"

"The others brought it with them when he first arrived."

"What others?"

"You went inside the bedroom. There were others the night Mohsin brought him."

"How many others?"

"Two or three."

"Three men to carry a small bundle of newspapers?"

"I tell you, I don't know anything about it. Anyway, I said I wouldn't deliver it."

"Why would he want you to deliver newspapers across town?"

"I don't know."

"Why would he keep newspapers with him in the cellar?" she asked insistently. "It's pitch dark down there."

"I tell you Jamilah, I don't know. It's not our business to know."

"If he's staying in our house then it is our business."

There was a pause. Sakina realised she had not thrown any water at the wall in a while. She hastily flung a couple of mugfuls. She tried to listen to the rest of the conversation, but could hear nothing. Aftab and Jamilah had either lowered their voices or moved out of earshot. She wondered whether her father was telling her mother about the young man's flirtation.

Sakina undressed and swiftly washed herself with the remaining water. A plan formed in her mind. It excited her. She wiped herself dry and critically examined herself in the small face mirror. Her nose was too large and her eyes were set too close together, she decided. Her mouth was not quite right, either. She turned sideways and looked at the mirror through the corner of one eye. She looked better in profile, but she did not think she was beautiful. She wondered if the young man in the cellar had been sincere about his compliment.

Aftab and Jamilah watched her carefully when she emerged from the bathroom. Sakina made a mental note to be more circumspect about her eavesdropping. She dressed for school, and packed her lunch-box. Her parents got ready to set off for the tailoring shop.

"Are you off to school?" Jamilah asked.

"Yes." Sakina stood at the door in her school uniform. Her knapsack was on her back.

"Have you had your lunch?"

Sakina patted her knapsack.

"Study hard," Jamilah said. "And if we are not home by the time you return, remember, you are not to have any conversation with him." Jamilah jerked her head in the direction of the cellar.

"Of course not," said Sakina in her most virtuous voice. "I know that curses befall the curious."

Sakina left the house. She ducked around the corner and concealed herself. In a few moments, she saw her parents emerge from the house and lock the door behind them. Aftab Ahsan turned his cap against the wind and Jamilah pulled her coat around herself. They hurried off in the opposite direction. Sakina watched them – they looked like small people with small dreams, scurrying about their small lives. She was glad she was not like them. They had no sense of the drama around them in Kashmir, the opportunities that the uprising afforded for heroism. Many of her classmates were involved in the freedom movement. The boys talked knowledgeably about guns and hideouts, and the girls talked familiarly about dalliances with handsome guerrillas. Sakina would listen quietly, knowing she was braver than any of them.

After waiting a few moments, she returned to the house and let herself in. She ran to her bedroom. For the first time since the fugitive arrived, she felt like she was doing something dangerous. She felt allied with him, allied in the cause of youth and adventure, allied against her parents and all they represented. She got out of her schoolgirl's uniform and put on the prettiest dress she owned. She applied lipstick, and donned bangles and earrings. She unpacked her own lunch, and put the food on a tray. She lit a candle and carried the tray to the cellar. Before she rapped on the trapdoor, she unwrapped her shawl and adjusted the necklace that her father had given her as a birthday present. She warmed her hands against the heat of the candle flame and pressed her palms against her cheeks to bring the blood to them. She knocked on the trapdoor. He opened it instantly, although it was unusual for anyone to bring him food at this time. It was as if he had been waiting for her.

He brought his face into the candlelight. He could not have been much older than twenty. She stared at him and wondered why her parents feared him.

"Got tired of your childish tricks?" she said, trying to sound as caustic as possible. "You've been hiding like a child whenever I came down."

He took in her excessive lipstick and jewellery and smiled. "I had not dared to show my face to someone so beautiful," he said.

"So why are you showing your face now? Have I become ugly?"

"No, it's just that you have found me out. What is the point of hiding any more?"

"I brought you some food," she said unnecessarily.

"Yes, I see that."

"Shall I come back later for the tray?"

She had never asked him that before. She had always waited until he had finished eating. She hoped that he would send her away so that he would not see her embarrassment and she hoped also that he would never send her away.

"I would rather you talked to me," he said.

"What do you want to talk about?"

"What is your name?" he asked softly.

"Sakina." It felt like an ugly name and she was ashamed to offer it to him.

"Sakina. A lovely name. A lovely name for a lovely girl."

She was not sure whether to believe him. She felt foolish and naive. She wanted to show that she was his equal. Yet, she felt uncharacteristically shy. Her breath came and went in little gasps. It was a strange sensation to be in his presence, one that was not altogether pleasant.

"You are not eating your food," she said. "I made this especially for you."

"Will you eat a little with me?"

She shook her head, but when he offered her a portion she took it and found that she was hungry. He laughed. His teeth were very white.

"Look at us sitting here and eating together," he said. "Just like husband and wife."

She flushed hotly. "I think it was better when you were hiding," Sakina said. "It would spare me from such stupid conversation."

"I can take bullets. But a harsh word from you can kill me."

"Enough with your foolishness – just eat your food," she commanded, sitting down on the floor and turning her head so that he could see her face in profile. She worried about the effect of the candlelight. It had the propensity to highlight flaws in her complexion.

He reached for the tray and began to eat, but his eyes did not leave her for a single moment.

"Don't look at me, look at your food," she said.

He inclined his head towards the food, but flirtatiously continued to look at her. Her heart sang.

"Did no one ever teach you to eat with your mouth closed?" she demanded.

"It isn't possible to close my mouth when you are around. It is in your nature to cause men to gape."

"No one wants to see what your food looks like after you have chewed it."

"For your sake, I swear I will always close my mouth when I eat. But you must permit me to stare at you."

"Heaven save me from your kind," she said, and sighed melodramatically, as she had seen many heroines do in innumerable movies. She daintily drew up her knees and rested her chin on them. She crossed her wrists around her ankles and made sure the light caught the bangles properly.

"What kind is that?" he asked.

"Mad and bad."

"I agree I'm mad for you. But I am not bad. I am good for you."

"Enough chit-chat. Are you done yet?"

"What's the hurry?"

"Unlike your Royal Highness who must be waited on hand and foot, I have work to do. I have to go to school—"

"If you will let me, I shall wait on you hand and foot."

"Yes, until you meet the next girl on the street."

"I swear, you are the only girl I will ever love."

"Imagine that. I don't even know your name. And you are talking about love."

"Love does not need a name," he said.

"All that is very well, but how will I distinguish you from my other lovers?"

He was taken aback and she was pleased to have

disconcerted him.

"My name is Basheer," he said.

She turned the word around in her mouth. It was a nice name.

"Basheer what? Don't you belong to a family?"

He shook his head. "I have no family. But I hope to start one soon since I have just met the girl of my dreams."

"It's a fine business you have got going. You travel from one house to the next, and others give you food and shelter, and you spend all your time flirting with all the innocent girls you find."

"Is that what you think I do?"

"It's a fine life, I must say. I'd like to get this kind of a job."

"You can't."

"Why not?"

"You have to be a young man in love."

"Well, oh young man in love, if you don't shut up and finish eating, I shall have to tell my father about you. Maybe my mother will be the one who starts bringing your meals."

"What would he say if you told him that we were in love?" he asked.

"First you ask him to walk across the city carrying your parcel and now you want to steal his daughter?" She addressed the comment to her own feet. She waited tensely. He stopped eating. He pushed the tray away.

"I see you have sharp ears," he said finally.

"Well –?" she said. "Isn't it true?"

"What if it is?"

"Maybe you asked the wrong person to perform your favour for you."

He studied her to see if she was joking. When he saw that she was serious, he gently took her hand. He stroked her wrist. It sent shivers of sensation down her spine.

"Would you do it for me?" he asked.

Every inch of her skin in contact with his fingers felt aflame.

"Maybe."

"What does it depend on?"

"What is it worth to you?"

He raised her wrist to his mouth and pressed his lips against it. She felt the coarseness of his stubble against her skin. Her heart skipped several beats.

"I give you my heart," he said. "Isn't that enough?"

"And yet you told my father that that you would leave as soon as this package was delivered."

"I didn't know then that you had the same feelings for me that I have for you."

"I don't," said Sakina, withdrawing her hand.

Basheer leaped up and started climbing the stairs.

"Where are you going?" asked Sakina in alarm.

"I'm going to give myself up to the police," he shouted. "If what you say is true, then my life is not worth living."

She shook her head disgustedly, although it was exactly the sort of grand gesture she liked. "Come back down and don't be a fool," she said.

He came back slowly and sat down opposite her. He stared into her eyes. His eyes were so dark that the black dots of his pupils were almost indistinguishable. She felt both helpless and masterful, out of control and in charge. She saw herself through his eyes and felt herself turn beautiful. He leaned forward and kissed her on the mouth. She was shocked and thrilled and remembered to resist only after he had finished.

"How dare you!" she exclaimed, wiping her mouth with the back of her hand. She could feel the sweetness of his lips in the very core of her body. "I trust you and you take advantage of me?"

He looked contrite and Sakina was pleased she had found a man who knew how to play his role properly.

"I swear I was not taking advantage of you," he said, placing his hand on his heart. "I swear I give my heart to you. If I offended you by kissing you, I'm sorry. I was carried away by your beauty. Your lips are like petals, your hands are as tender as the mist. I could watch your hips all day and night and never need food or water."

"I suppose you think my hair is ordinary," she pouted.

"Your hair is so lovely that I want to breathe its fragrance the rest of my life."

He opened a switchblade, placed the knife at his finger and made a nick. Crimson drops fell on the floor. She gasped. She cupped her hands to catch the precious drops. Tears came to her eyes. He stroked her hair and recited:

How strange is blood; On the field of battle, it is spilled for hate; But in the garden of the heart, these drops mean love.

She rested her head against his chest and closed her eyes.

"Will you deliver it today?" he whispered.

She stiffened and opened her eyes doubtfully. Before she could say anything, he kissed her again.

* * * * *

In the late afternoon, after a great many caresses and a great many kisses, Basheer explained to Sakina what he wanted her to do with the package. She felt confused and overwhelmed by his ardour. The sensation of his fingers on her skin had filled her, and crowded everything else out. She had not allowed him to remove her inner garments, but his hands had travelled where his eyes had not, and the strangeness and wonder of the emotions she felt brought her to tears. She clung to him, and listened to his beating heart, and prayed he loved her as she loved him. She listened to his instructions, but they were difficult to remember. What would her parents say if they found out about her illicit encounter? She decided not to think about it. She focused on his voice and pressed herself against his chest once more. The cellar felt cold. She shivered. He made her repeat aloud the address where she was to deliver the package, and he told her what to say if she was accosted by a soldier or a policeman.

"Go," he said, "go now before your parents return. Bring me word of your success when you come with dinner tonight."

"Do you love me?" she asked.

"Of course," he replied. "I would not trust so dangerous a mission to someone I could not depend on."

It was not the answer she wanted, but she clung to it. She slipped out of the house with the package concealed under her coat.

It began to snow and the coat felt thin and useless against the bite of the wind. The sky was so overcast that darkness seemed to come quicker than usual. Sakina hugged the package to her heart to keep herself warm, but it was metallic and cold. She shivered, but felt the warmth of adventure. She passed figures on the street and did not look at them. She saw only their boots, and once they had passed, she saw their footprints in the snow — outlines that swiftly faded as the snow filled them out with whiteness. Sakina knew the city well. She knew the way to the address that Basheer had given her, and could have gone there in pitch darkness. It would have taken her only about an hour in the usual circumstances, but Basheer had given her detailed instructions on which intersections to avoid and where the police and military were likely to have roving search patrols. She took side roads where there was little chance of meeting other pedestrians and alleys that were too small for traffic. As the weather worsened, the streets grew silent and still. Through alley after alley, she didn't see another soul. In the distance at one point, under the light of a street lamp, she saw an army truck. She ducked into a ditch and waited for it to leave. It was in the middle of an intersection close to the army barracks. She had to cross it to get to the address Basheer had given her. At first, the truck seemed abandoned, and then, just as she was getting ready to risk walking by it, a dirty spout of exhaust emerged from its innards. Like an animal emerging from hibernation, it turned one way and then another and finally blundered away in the direction of the barracks. Sakina waited until the snow had filled out the tracks of the tires, and then she got out of the ditch and continued on her way. By now, her fingers had lost all sensation. She could tell that she held the package only because its jagged edge cut against her chest. She was afraid she would drop it. She pressed it fiercely against herself. There was snow under her collar. Flakes hung on her eyelashes. Her cheeks felt so numb that she was not sure she was capable of speech. It was very dark and the snow muffled all sound. Sakina thought of being home in Basheer's arms, safe and warm. The thought spurred her final few steps to the address he had given her. Six logs of wood stood beside a weather-beaten brown door, just as Basheer had said.

Sakina knocked. She heard a rustling sound that was followed by silence and she could not tell whether the sound had come from the wind or from inside the house. She knocked again. The door opened a crack.

"Who is it?" a deep male voice asked.

"A friend of Basheer," stammered Sakina through lips caked with cold. "I am looking for Iqbal."

The door opened slowly. Sakina stepped inside. She tried

to adjust her eyes to the pitch blackness. The man who opened the door struck a match. She gasped. She was in a small room, barely larger than her bedroom. There were at least twenty men pressed against each other in that little space and several of them held automatic rifles. Many seemed ready to start shooting.

"Basheer sent me," she said. Her voice shook.

The men took in the smudged lipstick on Sakina's bloodless face. Several laughed quietly. They took their hands off their weapons.

"Trust Basheer to get his whores to do his work for him," said a man in the corner. There was more laughter. Sakina felt a flare of rage. The man who had opened the door waved the men silent.

"Did he send a package?" he asked.

Sakina opened her coat and gave the man the bundle. He took it gingerly with both hands, handling it with a delicacy that she had not thought to exercise.

"Very good," he said.

The man in the corner addressed Sakina: "Did Basheer pay you enough to service some of his friends?"

There was more laughter. Sakina's eyes flashed.

"I'm not a prostitute," she said. Then, because of the disbelieving expressions on the faces of the men, she added, "Basheer is going to marry me."

There were whoops of mirth at this. "When is the wedding?" asked another man.

"How many other brides will be at the ceremony?"

"Didn't Basheer tell you he shares everything with his brothers?"

"You don't know anything," Sakina retorted angrily. Her outburst was greeted by more merriment. The man who had opened the door silenced the men.

"You had better go," he told Sakina. "Be careful not to be followed."

The thought of stepping out into the cold dismayed her. "Can you spare me a dry towel and a cap?" she asked.

The men thought this was funny, as well. "No," said the man, opening the door. "We have none to spare."

"Ask Basheer for the cap," advised another voice. "It's the least he can do for his future wife."

Sakina did not reply. She gathered herself with as much dignity as she could muster and stepped outside. Behind her, the men bid her farewell by making kissing and sucking sounds.

The wind slapped her in the face. She gasped. She involuntarily started to shiver. She felt drained of energy. She was not sure she could make it home. The thought of the lengthy detour Basheer had instructed her to follow demoralised her. She was sure she would end up in a ditch. They would find her the next day, frozen solid. It was better to risk the soldiers and the patrols she might encounter on the direct route. Maybe they would even take her home. No, she remembered, she couldn't ask them to take her home. She was in league with a fugitive. What would the men in the house do with the package she had delivered? Sakina realised she had not thought this far. She had simply done as Basheer had asked. The comments of his friends had upset her. Could they have been right? Was Basheer just using her? She thought of his dark eyes and his fervent pleas of love and she dismissed such fears as unworthy. He had spilled his own blood and kissed her tenderly. Surely it meant he loved her. The snow fell and the wind howled. Sakina approached the intersection where she had seen the army truck. She observed the area from behind a tree. The storm had grown so violent that it had apparently driven the soldiers back into the barracks. The intersection seemed deserted. She pulled the coat a little tighter around herself and stepped into the street.

Her head was tucked so low that it was the soldier's boots she saw first, although they were covered with snow and almost invisible. She looked up and saw a man detach himself from the darkness. He was almost entirely coated in white, and even the darkness of his moustache and his eyebrows were wreathed in snowflakes. He could have been a ghost, except that his eyes were coal black. Sakina spent one moment incongruously reflecting that they reminded her of Basheer's eyes. Then she took in the automatic rifle he carried and the contrast of its blue-black sheen against the absolute whiteness of the snow. It seemed like an instrument of pure terror and she shrieked and instinctively turned and ran. He caught her before she had taken a dozen steps. He tackled her with a degree of force that was unnecessary given the difference in their sizes.

"Whore," he said through clenched teeth. "What are you doing near the barracks?"

Sakina could not answer because the soldier had pinned her neck into the snow with his elbow. She flailed ineffectually at him, but her blows had barely the strength of a child. The heat of suffocation spread out from her lungs and engulfed her until the soldier abruptly eased up.

"I was lost," she gasped. There was a constriction in her throat and the words sounded raspy and choked. She coughed violently.

"Liar!"

He slapped her hard across the face. Blood spurted from her nose. He grabbed her hand and yanked her to her feet in one motion. He frisked her roughly, running his gloved hands down her sides. He twisted one of her arms behind her back and pushed her ahead of him.

"Where are you taking me?" she asked, but her words were lost in the howling wind.

He led her around a culvert and she saw the same truck she had spotted earlier. It was draped in white and seemed frozen. The soldier rapped on the door on the driver's side and a sergeant opened it. A blast of warm air leaped out at Sakina. The sergeant was smoking a cigarette.

"She was acting suspicious, sir," the soldier told the sergeant. "I apprehended her down the road, near the main intersection."

The sergeant stared at Sakina. He seemed annoyed that she had caused him to have to open the door of the truck.

"Handcuff her and get in," he said shortly, sliding over to the passenger seat. "We'll take her to headquarters."

The soldier locked Sakina's wrists behind her and bodily

lifted her into the cabin. He jumped in behind her. Sakina found herself pressed tightly between the torsos of the two men. The soldier who had apprehended Sakina drove the truck. The sergeant sucked on his cigarette and blew smoke at the windshield.

"What was she doing?," the sergeant asked finally.

"Acting suspicious, sir. She tried to run when I intercepted her."

"They are all swine."

"Yes, sir."

"What were you doing?," the sergeant asked Sakina.

"I was lost."

The sergeant blew some more smoke. "Better start telling the truth when you get to headquarters," he advised in a friendly manner, addressing himself to the windshield. "Headquarters doesn't like whores who tell lies."

Sakina thought of Basheer waiting for her in the cellar. Bring me word of your success when you come with dinner tonight, he had said. How could she tell him that she had succeeded, that she had proved equal to his challenge, that she was worthy of his love? The truck bumped over the potholes and skidded over patches of ice.

At the entrance to the barracks, the soldier who apprehended Sakina stopped the truck about thirty feet from the gate. He got out of the truck and approached the guard-tower with his hands raised. A spotlight from the tower was trained on the soldier, and then on the truck. Sakina was blinded, and turned her face to one side. The gate of the barracks swung open and the solider came running back to the truck, eased it into gear and drove into a courtyard. The gate closed behind them.

"Get out," the sergeant told Sakina. He was still smoking.

The soldier lifted Sakina onto the ground. The courtyard was flanked by a series of tightly-packed, low-slung barracks. Men in uniform were visible everywhere. The soldier gave her a push. Sakina stumbled along, sniffling against the biting cold and her fear.

"You've no right to be doing this –" she began, but was cut off by a swift jab between the shoulder blades. She stumbled, and without her arms for balance, she fell. She tasted dirt and snow.

"Get up." The soldier's boot nudged her in the side. "Get up and shut up."

She struggled upright. They passed by several barracks and came to a larger building at the end, which looked like it had once been a residential mansion. Through a door at the side, they entered a large hall. There was a single desk in the centre. The soldier held Sakina's arm above the elbow and propelled her to the desk. A bearded man sat behind it. He eyed Sakina from head to toe and looked at the soldier questioningly.

"We found this whore outside the barracks. She was acting suspicious."

"I'm not a whore," Sakina shouted. "I was just lost –"

The soldier pressed down on her handcuffs, throwing back Sakina's shoulders and sending an arc of pain through her back.

"You're not a whore?" the bearded man behind the desk asked.

"No." She spoke through clenched teeth.

"What are you then?

"I'm a schoolgirl."

"I see." The soldier eased up on Sakina.

"What is your name?" the bearded man asked.

"Sakina."

"Father's name?"

"Aftab Ahsan." The moment she said the words, Sakina realised that she might have compromised Basheer's safety. Mentally, she cursed herself.

"Where do you live?" the bearded man asked.

"Right here in Srinagar."

"Address?"

"Why do I have to tell you anything?" she asked defiantly.

"Why would an ordinary schoolgirl want to hide her address?"

She glared at him. "It's none of your business, that's why."

"Don't you want us to take you home?"

She glared at him. "I can find my way back."

"You said you were lost."

She had no answer. He smiled, and it infuriated Sakina that he was toying with her.

"Now tell me where you live and what you were doing outside the barracks?"

She bit her lip and remained silent.

"Why would an innocent schoolgirl refuse to answer such simple questions?"

She assumed her most steely expression.

"Nobody keeps secrets here," he said quietly. "No one. And some of the others won't ask nicely, like I am doing."

A sob escaped Sakina. Her eyes filled with tears. What had she done? Why had she been so foolish? She wished she had listened to Aftab and Jamilah, and gone to school like any other schoolgirl. But then she remembered Basheer's words, his look and the touch of his hands. She had wanted to do this favour for him, she had sought it out herself. It had seemed easy, the quickest way to show him that she was worthy of his affections. And now, now she was on the verge of ruining everything.

"I'm asking you for the last time," the bearded man said. "Let me tell you what I think. I don't think you were lost. I think you were doing something outside the barracks, something you shouldn't have been doing. No one wanders into this part of the city in the middle of a snow storm because they are lost. If you talk, things will be better for you."

Still sobbing, Sakina remembered Basheer's words: "Bring me word of your success when you come with dinner tonight." She would not be bringing him his dinner, nor word of her success. But succeed she had, even if she could not tell him so.

The bearded man sighed. "Take her inside," he told the soldier, and turned away.

The soldier roughly escorted her to a side door and down a set of steps. They passed sentries and guards. There was a narrow corridor and a series of cells. The soldier took Sakina to the last cell. A sentry unlocked it. The soldier removed Sakina's handcuffs and escorted her inside.

"Remove your clothes," he said without expression.

"What? How dare you —"

"Prisoners are not allowed to have their own clothing."

"What will I wear?"

The soldier indicated a narrow ledge inside the cell, a slab of stone that served as a bed. A shirt and a pair of trousers lay next to a sheet and a pillow.

"No," she said.

"You can remove them or I can remove them for you." He took a step towards her. She shrank to the corner of the cell, screaming. He waited for her to catch her breath.

"Scream as loud as you like," he said, in the informative manner of a travel guide. "Louder the better."

He took another step towards her and Sakina succumbed.

She took off her shoes and the wet coat. She lifted the pretty dress she had worn for Basheer over her head and shoulders. Turning away from the soldier, she removed her undergarments.

"Such shyness for a whore," the soldier said, with a laugh. The sentry who had unlocked the cell stood by the bars, watching intently.

"This one I am going to enjoy," the sentry said.

The soldier laughed again. "I'll make the announcement at dinner. Tonight we are all going to have dessert."

Sakina grabbed the clothes on the ledge. She put them on quickly. They were several sizes too large, but she was grateful to cover her nakedness. The soldier picked up Sakina's clothes and left the cell. He stood by the bars as the sentry locked the cell.

"I haven't done anything," Sakina sobbed. "What are they going to do? What will they do to me?"

"You'll find out soon enough," the soldier said.

She collapsed onto the stone ledge. She was cold, exhausted and at the edge of despair. Her parents would have returned home to find her missing. Would they think to ask Basheer where she was? Would he tell them? She curled into a fetal position. She wished she had listened to Basheer's advice and taken the roundabout route back home. Between the soldiers, the cold and the snow, she preferred the storm. It would have been better to have ended up in a ditch, frozen, than endure what the soldiers might inflict on her. For a second, she imagined Basheer storming the army barracks and freeing her. She saw him unlocking the cell door and carrying her away to a life of freedom and adventure. But that could not happen. He did not even know where she was. She imagined him in the cellar, pining for her, and resolved to stay true to him. He had promised her eternal love, and she would do the same for him. She huddled a little tighter into herself. She wrapped her arms around her knees and obtained a little warmth. She was very tired and, in spite of herself, slipped into a dreamless sleep.

◆

There was a shriek. It came from far away, high-pitched and terrible, and it cut through the night like a scythe. She awoke, instantly alert. She was not sure how long she had slept. And then the ground shook and there was a deafening explosion that shook the walls of the cell. Sakina toppled onto the floor. The lights went out. There were cries from the other cells. The explosion left a ringing sound in her ears and Sakina knew with a terrible certainty that the package she had delivered for Basheer had been an instrument of immense destruction. She screamed. Lying in the dark on the hard ground, she could not reconcile the dashing image of Basheer with the horror that he had wrought through her. This was her doing as well as his, the explosion was the murderous result of their illicit love – she was certain of that. She felt guilt and fear. But the regret did not cancel out her love. What he had done through her was monstrous, but the monstrosity was not within him, it could not have been in his hands and eyes and chest, not in his voice, not in his promises of love.

There were alarms and shouts and running feet. Sakina heard a sentry shout that the main mess hall had been hit and that the casualties were heavy. She steeled herself for what she knew was coming. It would only take moments for someone to connect her presence near the barracks to the explosion.

She was right. The soldier who had apprehended her outside the barracks was the first to return. He shone a flashlight through the bars. "Fucking whore!" he shouted. Sakina shrank away. In seconds, there were more flashlights.

"In the last cell!" someone shouted.

The cell door was unlocked. A flashlight swung in a crazy arc and Sakina felt a powerful blow knock her sideways. Rough hands gripped her by the front of her shirt. The buttons tore open. She screamed, and was silenced by another blow.

"Whore!"

Boots pounded her ribs.

"Swine!"

She tasted blood in her mouth.

"Please," she screamed. "Please stop."

There was a commotion in the corridor. Someone shouted "Captain Chawla!" The soldiers with the flashlights stepped back, but kept the lights trained on her. A man stepped into the cell, accompanied by the bearded man who had questioned her earlier. In the glow of the flashlights, Sakina could see Captain Chawla was powerfully built. There were cuts on his face and he was bleeding.

"What do we know about her?" he asked.

The bearded man spoke: "Her name is Sakina. Father's name is Aftab Ahsan."

"What else?" Captain Chawla asked.

The soldier who had apprehended Sakina said, "I captured her outside the barracks about two hours ago, sir."

"What has she revealed during interrogation? Where does she live?"

There were shuffled feet and silence.

"She has not yet been interrogated?"

"We were waiting for the men to finish dinner," said the bearded man.

"Fools!" shouted Captain Chawla. "I am working with fools. We are in the middle of a war and you delay in interrogating a dangerous guerrilla? We have more than sixty casualties." He pointed at Sakina. "Because of her."

Another soldier came running up the corridor. He was out of breath, but snapped to attention.

"Yes?" said Captain Chawla.

"It was probably someone from Basheer Ahmed's group, sir. Intelligence reported that he entered the area last week."

Captain Chawla pounded a fist against his palm. "The swine," he roared. "I'm going to kill the bastard with my own hands."

"We are working all the channels," the soldier continued. "About a week ago, we had a reported sighting of him near Kalima Street."

Sakina gasped. Captain Chawla whirled.

"Tell me!" he shouted. "What do you know about this?"

She shook her head, struck mute with fear. Captain Chawla unholstered a gun and placed it at her temple.

"You have three seconds," he said, flicking off the safety catch. "Do you live on Kalima Street?"

She stared wide-eyed. "One!" Captain Chawla said. "Two!"

The terror surged inside her and she nodded.

"Where?" he asked.

She was helpless. Hating herself, she said, "behind the mosque."

Captain Chawla lowered his gun. Without taking his eyes off Sakina, he commanded, "get a jeep." He turned away. "She comes with me."

The soldiers handcuffed Sakina and marched her out of the cell. Outside in the courtyard, two of the barracks were burning. The night was filled with chaos. Debris was strewn everywhere and fire engines were dousing the flames. Men rushed about screaming vengeance and rage. A few women wandered vacantly, some had tears streaming down their faces.

The soldiers loaded Sakina into the back of a jeep. Captain Chawla got in. Soldiers climbed in after him.

"Kalima Street," Captain Chawla commanded. The vehicle pulled away.

The jeep cut through narrow alleys. Men in khaki were already fanning out. The sentries snapped to attention as the jeep careened past.

"What is the door number?" Captain Chawla asked Sakina.

She shook her head.

"What was that?" said Captain Chawla.

"You are not getting any more information from me."

Captain Chawla swallowed. One of the soldiers in the front seat unholstered his gun.

"That won't be necessary," said Captain Chawla. "I've thought of another way."

In a little while, the jeep made a hard left turn and pulled onto the block of Kalima Street behind the mosque.

"Where should I stop?" asked the driver.

"In the middle of the street," replied Captain Chawla.

When the jeep came to a halt, Captain Chawla leaped out. He dragged Sakina onto the road and shoved her down onto her knees. He clicked the safety off his revolver and fired a shot into the air. The report was deafening. It echoed off the walls of houses. Lights in a couple of windows came on and then were immediately switched off.

"I am looking for Aftab Ahsan's house," bellowed Captain Chawla. His voice was so loud that the other soldiers could hear its echo spread through the neighbourhood. "We have your daughter, Sakina. Open the door or the next bullet goes into her head."

A look of admiration sprang into the eyes of the soldiers. Sakina realised what was happening and screamed: "No–!"

But the front door of a house had already opened. Aftab Ahsan and Jamilah emerged and they already had their palms folded in submission.

"Spare her, master," the man begged. "We thought she was lost."

"She is only a child," said Jamilah.

Captain Chawla bellowed in triumph. With the soldiers behind him he ran towards the house. He roughly pushed aside the tailor and his wife and entered the living room. He turned to the two soldiers who had accompanied him. "Search the cellar."

Aftab and Jamilah ran towards Sakina to pick her up, but she was already on her feet. She was jabbering incoherently. Before they could stop her, she ran past them into the house.

"Basheer!" she screamed. "Basheer, they are coming for you!"

She entered the house just as Captain Chawla emerged from the bedroom. Two shots rang out from the cellar. Captain Chawla whirled and dropped to one knee, his revolver at the ready. The door from the cellar flew open and Basheer sprang out, gun in hand. Before either man could fire, Sakina flung herself at Captain Chawla, knocking him off-balance.

"Sakina–" screamed her father in fear and disbelief.

Basheer seized his chance and raced for the front door. Captain Chawla recovered his footing and fired but missed.

There were shots outside and cries.

Sakina lay on the ground and cried out, "Basheer, Basheer!"

Captain Chawla ran to the door and saw that his quarry had escaped him. He roared with anger.

"Whore!" he shouted at Sakina. He swung his fist and caught her across the jaw. He grabbed her by the throat and yanked her upright.

"Please don't," begged Aftab Ahsan.

"She is only fourteen–" said Jamilah.

Sakina spat at Captain Chawla's face. He pushed her away, levelled his gun and fired once into her chest. He strode out without closing the door, and a cold gust blew through the house. Aftab Ahsan and Jamilah rushed to their daughter.

"My jewel, my darling!" Aftab Ahsan cried. A dark pool of crimson seeped onto the floor.

Jamilah held her daughter's hands. "Please, please, God," she prayed. "Please spare her."

It had never been clearer to Sakina how much her parents loved her. She wanted to tell them how much she loved them, too, but she lacked the will. In only a few moments, she fell silent.

The Gentleman's Game

At the height of the border war between India and Pakistan, chance and caprice caused the two countries to be pitted against each other in the finals of the World Cup cricket tournament. Six time zones from the icy battlefront, eleven players from each country met to do battle on a lush green field in England.

Across the subcontinent, several hundred million people huddled around television sets. Broadcasters in India and Pakistan, concerned about appearing frivolous, were initially hesitant to cut away from their war coverage to televise the cricket match, but it quickly became apparent that for most viewers there was little difference between the two programmes.

"Cricket in India and Pakistan has always been taken seriously, but perhaps never more so than today," said a former captain of the Indian team from the central commentary booth. "Great things are expected from this crack Indian side. Its arsenal is large and its firepower tremendous. Pakistan would do well to strap on its helmet."

From the other end of the commentary table, a former captain of the Pakistan team said: "We've been hearing about crack Indian teams for decades. It makes sense, since the Indians have always cracked under pressure. Bookies are giving Pakistan two to one odds because the team has the world's two fastest bowlers. If it's war that India wants, it's war that India will get."

The Prime Minister's office in India issued a press release minutes before the game began: "Our brave soldiers are succeeding in throwing back the terrorists from the Motherland. Earlier today, we succeeded in capturing Panther Hill at an altitude of eight thousand feet. We hope the approach of total victory on the battlefront will boost the morale of our cricket team in England."

The statement was read and repeated frequently on international satellite TV. As the cricket captains stepped onto the field for the coin toss ceremony, Islamabad issued a statement of its own: "Panther Hill is still very much under our control. The slopes are drenched in the blood of the Indian oppressors and our freedom fighters have captured many prisoners. It is to be hoped that India will pause and reconsider its misadventure in Kashmir. If not, we expect the same result in war as we expect from the upcoming cricket match."

The truth was mixed: The peak of Panther Hill was still in Pakistani hands, but an Indian takeover was imminent. The massive Indian attacks – shelling from below and bombs from above – had wiped out the main Pakistani strongholds. The Pakistanis now held the peak with rifles and small arms fire. As darkness fell, the treacherous slopes became impassable. Pakistani snipers with infrared gun sights could pick out Indians hundreds of feet below. The Indian heavy guns had to be silenced since Indian soldiers were themselves so close to the peak. The Indians dug in behind a ridge seven hundred feet below the peak and waited for air support to arrive at daybreak.

The soldiers from both sides were as passionately interested in the cricket match as everyone else. They huddled around radios. When India won the coin toss, the Indian soldiers behind the ridge loosed a volley of shots into the night. Up on the peak, the Pakistanis first thought the Indians had begun a suicidal night attack and they responded with mad fire. When the snow settled, it became clear that not a single Indian helmet had poked out from behind the ridge.

Major Asif Masood from the 12th Pakistan Frontier Regiment played his infrared binoculars slowly along the length of the ridge. Nothing but snow and ice and wind. Behind him, a low snigger came from the huddle of men sitting on the ground around a radio and a heater. It was the Indian prisoner, the man who had been captured by an ambush team earlier that day, after he had got to one hundred feet from the peak. An interrogation revealed he was twenty-two-year-old Corporal Pranlal of the Fourth Indian Rifles Regiment.

Major Masood made his way to the little group. He was a burly man with the perpetually suspicious expression of the veteran soldier. Words came slowly to him, unless he was under fire or very drunk, when they came in a rush. His cheeks and chin sported a two-week old beard and the dark circles under his eyes made them seem hooded. He towered over the Indian. The prisoner's wrists were bound behind his back. Corporal Pranlal twisted his shoulders and looked at Major Masood insolently.

"It was the coin toss," the Indian corporal said. "India won the toss."

The Pakistani Major stroked his beard with the back of his fingers.

"The pitch at Lords is key," Corporal Pranlal continued, in the manner of someone addressing friends over a pitcher of beer. "By the time Pakistan gets to bat, it will turn like a top."

The Pakistani soldiers guarding Corporal Pranlal looked

at Major Masood for direction. Niaz Ahmed, the twenty-year-old private who was closest to the Indian, was anxious to speak: It was true that the pitch at Lords made Pakistan's batting difficult, but it also made the Pakistani pace bowling deadly. Major Masood continued to stroke his beard. Young Ahmed could contain himself no longer.

"We wanted to bowl first anyway," he said.

There were murmurs of agreement from the other Pakistani soldiers. It was true – the Pakistani captain had said so before the match. Corporal Pranlal's eyes flashed.

"Bowl first at Lords? You're crazy."

Major Masood's fist flashed out and struck the Indian corporal behind the ear. His head snapped to the side and, because he could not move his arms to balance himself, he toppled over. The others slowly helped him sit up.

"Crazy? Crazy, you say?" Major Masood said and he punched Corporal Pranlal again. A scarlet trickle of blood erupted at the corner of the Indian's mouth. "Swine, I can kill you for being insolent."

Ahmed, the Pakistani private, bit his lip. It certainly was insolent of the Indian prisoner to have called him crazy, but Major Masood should not have slapped him. Cricket was a gentleman's game and everyone was entitled to his opinion. If Corporal Pranlal were wrong, the match would prove it.

"You know, you're wrong," the Pakistani private ventured to the Indian prisoner, as a way to signal to his commander that the slap was misplaced. "The match will prove it."

The Pakistani major glared at his subordinate, who

clenched his jaws and glared right back. When the Pakistani private did not back down, Major Masood turned back to the Indian prisoner.

"So you like cricket?" he asked Corporal Pranlal, in a voice that was falsely conversational.

The Indian nodded. He was afraid.

"How sure are you about the cricket pitch?"

The Indian corporal hesitated. When he spoke, his voice was quiet: "I'm sure."

Major Masood unholstered his gun, placed the barrel at Corporal Pranlal's temple, and flicked off the safety catch.

"Pray that you were wrong," he said.

*   *   *   *   *

The Pakistani bowlers struck blood early, and sent the first Indian batsman back to the pavilion. The little knot of Pakistani soldiers fired their guns into the air. When the next Indian batsman struck the ball around the ground, the Indian soldiers behind the ridge fired in celebration. So it went, alternate bursts of gunfire punctuating the night. The stars rose over the mountain, so bright they appeared to have crept closer to earth to watch the game. In distant England, players flung themselves around the field with a ferocity that they had not displayed before in the tournament. The stakes were much higher than a mere cup; victory had taken on moral hues. The winning side would be feted and celebrated back home; the losers would be pilloried, accused of selling out, perhaps threatened with death.

Major Masood detached himself from the band of soldiers

guarding Corporal Pranlal and returned to scanning the slopes. The remaining soldiers were all youngsters and, with their commanding officer gone, their mood lightened. The Indian corporal, sombre after Major Masood's threat, found himself relieved that things were not going as well for the Indian cricketers as he had expected.

"Quack, quack, quack," Private Ahmed told Corporal Pranlal, as the Pakistani bowlers dismissed an Indian batsman for a duck. The Indian soldier grinned sheepishly.

"Bad umpiring," Corporal Pranlal told the Pakistani private, after another Indian batsman was dismissed.

"There was no question about it," the Pakistani responded. "He was out."

It seemed at first that Ahmed had been right – the pitch favoured the Pakistani fast bowlers. Indian batsmen came and went in a steady stream as the ball bounced and reared. It seemed as if Pakistan would have an easy win.

"Who said batting first was going to be easy?" asked Private Ahmed innocently, with a triumphant expression and a sideways glance at Corporal Pranlal.

"Don't count your chickens before they are hatched," the Indian corporal admonished. "The game isn't over yet."

The Pakistani soldiers yelled and shouted. They fired shots into the air and even loosed off a flare, which brightly lit the mountain slopes for an instant.

Major Masood approached the group when the din grew too loud.

"Do not forget that we are at war," he said. The soldiers fell silent, like errant schoolboys before a headmaster.

Major Masood nudged Corporal Pranlal with his knee and laughed: "It seems as if your prayers for the Pakistani side are working. Keep up the good work."

Corporal Pranlal did not reply. He was secretly glad that the Indian side was losing. As the stars passed overhead, the soldiers brewed tea. Private Ahmed held a cup to Corporal Pranlal's lips so he too could drink. When some tea dribbled onto the Indian corporal's chin, the Pakistani private brushed it off with the back of a gloved hand, taking care not to scrape the dark clot of red at the corner of the prisoner's mouth. Ahmed placed a cigarette between Corporal Pranlal's lips and held a light for him. With the players in England taking a break, the little group on the mountain fell silent. The sweet smell of tea, the aroma of tobacco and the crackling radio felt warm and good. The stars dotted the sky in a thousand different patterns whose meanings each soldier interpreted differently. The men sat and rocked and smoked and thought. Major Masood was back to scanning the slopes for a surprise Indian attack.

Just before the game resumed, the Indian corporal turned to Private Ahmed.

"Do you think he will do it?" Corporal Pranlal asked, nodding his head in major Masood's direction. He could not bring himself to say the word, "kill."

Private Ahmed hesitated. Major Masood was certainly capable of killing the Indian soldier. Besides, by making so public a threat before his subordinates, he had left himself little choice but to carry it out. No officer could afford to lose face with the men he commanded.

"Why are you worrying?" Private Ahmed said with mock confidence. "India is going to lose."

The answer did not satisfy Corporal Pranlal and the next few minutes of the game proved that he was right to be concerned. Three Pakistani batsmen got out as the ball spun and ducked. The game was on. It was to be a match for the history books. Across the subcontinent, millions of people before thousands of television sets leaped together each time a ball was dispatched to the boundary or another batsman was declared out.

"Howzatt?" the Indians cried, each time the Pakistan batsmen floundered. They flung their arms in the air, in the traditional appeal to the umpire.

"Howzatt?" Corporal Pranlal echoed on the mountain peak, but in a half-hearted voice. He couldn't fling his hands in the air since they were bound behind his back, but his shoulders heaved. The Pakistani soldiers understood the gesture clearly enough. They also understood why he was half-hearted.

"You see, I was right," Corporal Pranlal observed, after another setback to the Pakistani team. He injected triumph into his voice when all he felt was fear.

"It's not over yet," replied Private Ahmed. He meant to say the words defiantly, but they came out sounding like reassurance.

"The Indian bowling is very good," said Corporal Pranlal. He was ashamed at himself for wishing that it wasn't.

"Yes, it is," said Private Ahmed. He placed a hand on the Indian's shoulder. "But the Pakistani batsmen are very good, too. Take heart, it is not over yet."

Every time there was a shout from the radio and another Pakistani batsman was dismissed, Major Masood's jaw muscles tightened. The Indian soldiers below the ridge loosed volley after volley of gunfire into the night, as the Pakistani soldiers on the peak grew ever more silent. Corporal Pranlal felt his throat go dry. His legs felt weak. Fear coursed through his body like a poison, threading its way through veins and arteries, pounding at his chest and throbbing at his temples. He reversed a lifetime of prayers on behalf of the Indian cricket team. He prayed the Indian bowlers would hit a poor spell, that the Pakistani batsmen would hold on, that a thunderstorm would wash out the match.

As the game progressed to its climax, the Pakistani cricketers floundered as the Indians grew increasingly ferocious. The Indian soldiers behind the ridge grew raucous and wild. The roar of their shouting carried up to the peak and the reports from their guns and flares were like fireworks. Each burst of gunfire sounded to Corporal Pranlal's ears like an execution squad. As the Pakistani batting collapsed and it became clear that India would win, Corporal Pranlal saw Major Masood approach. The eyes of the Pakistani major seethed with anger. He reached for his holster.

Corporal Pranlal turned to the Pakistani private. His eyes were wild with terror.

"Help me," he said, as the radio crackled. "Do something."

Private Ahmed gestured helplessly. His eyes, too, were filled with fear.

"At least untie my wrists," the Indian pleaded. "Give me a chance—"

There was a wild shout from the radio and then the commentary was drowned out by sustained gunfire from the Indian soldiers behind the ridge. Machine gun fire kicked up the snow and so many flares were fired that it seemed for a moment that the sun had begun to rise.

✦

The Indian planes came at daybreak, flying in dense formations. They passed over the peak but did not drop their bombs: The Pakistanis were gone.

Within minutes, Indian soldiers were racing up the mountain to the peak, yelling and shouting. One or two had discarded their helmets in favour of cricket caps. When they reached the peak they found a kettle with frozen tea and a dying radio. An Indian soldier lay twenty feet away, face down in the snow. His posture suggested he had been running when he fell. There was a halo of red around his head and his arms were flung above him, in the traditional cricketing gesture of appeal.

Major Mishra's Secret

He felt a flutter in his chest at a critical moment in the discussion, a tap-tap-tapping at his heart, like a message in Morse code. Instinctively he tried to decode it, before realising that it was unlikely to match any of the ciphers he had learned during his many years in the military. He waited for it to repeat, but it was silent.

General Ashok Pratap sat motionless in his chair. His feet remained solidly planted on the floor and his hands stayed on the conference table in a manner that suggested that he was holding it down. Half rolled sleeves exposed his bulging forearms. Other than a moment of insecurity that fleetingly crossed his face, nothing changed. But that was enough. The Prime Minister of Pakistan smiled ever so slightly. Without preamble, he said:

"Gentlemen, it seems we have reached agreement."

General Pratap's assistant, Major Arjun Mishra, choked and immediately disguised his reaction with a discreet cough. They had not reached agreement. They were not even close to agreement! The Pakistani side had come to the conference with a list of outrageous demands, which was absurd given their ruined state on the battlefield. Thousands of Indian soldiers had died in order to bring the Pakistanis to this conference table near the border, in order to allow General Pratap to dictate the terms of peace. Agreement? Even according to the etiquette of bluff, that was insane. Major Mishra kept his eyes focused on the Pakistani Prime Minister and waited for his commander to speak. But General Pratap said nothing. The silence grew until it filled every crevice in the room, until it became an answer in itself, an answer of capitulation and acquiescence. Major Mishra frowned. What was General Pratap thinking? He had staked his military career on leading the Indian forces into battle, taking the gravest risks in order to achieve total victory. Now, at the moment of triumph, he was refusing to drive home the advantage.

"War is a terrible business," said the Pakistani Prime Minister, now smiling broadly. "It is good that we are men of peace who wish to end it."

Major Mishra ventured a sideways glance. General Pratap's lips opened and closed once, but no sound issued from them. "Like a fish," Major Mishra thought, before he dismissed the thought as unworthy of his hero.

"I have the papers ready," said the Pakistani army's chief of staff. "If you will just sign here—"

Aides scurried around the room, ferrying papers from one end of the conference table to the other. Major Mishra considered moving his boot to nudge General Pratap's foot under the table, but could not bring himself to do so. It was never proper to kick a commanding officer. There had been other times when General Pratap had done the unexpected. Perhaps he had some grand plan under his sleeve. This was India's best-loved son, her bravest. "Pratap, the lion-hearted," the newspapers called him. Posters bearing his chiselled features were on bedroom walls across India, hero-worshipped by teenage boys and adored by their sisters. No, General Pratap would never let his country down—

Abruptly, without any outward sign of anguish, General

Pratap's torso tipped forward. His forehead hit the table with a crack that made Major Mishra wince. The General's lips fell on the papers that the aides had placed before him, so that it seemed as if he was kissing the Pakistani offer.

So ingrained was Major Mishra's training that he refused to come to the aid of his commander. Everything he had learned over three decades of service indicated that General Pratap was invincible and immortal. He was immune to disease, delirium and distress. He never did anything that he had not himself willed. General Pratap never needed help.

It was the Pakistani Prime Minister who first shouted, "fetch a doctor!" Pakistani officers and orderlies rushed forward to lift General Pratap. Major Mishra leaped up to fight them before he realised that they were doing the right thing. Together, they lifted the general. His face had turned ashen and his eyes were closed. He was not breathing. There was a trickle of blood at his lip. Within moments, paramedics rushed in and manoeuvred General Pratap onto a stretcher. As they carried him out, Major Mishra noticed that the general's bloody lips had left their outline on the papers the Pakistanis had placed before him.

*   *   *   *   *

From the start, Major Mishra had had misgivings about conducting the secret negotiations on Pakistani soil. It was a concession that General Pratap had agreed to in return for the Pakistani Prime Minister's presence at the talks. The General had been so eager to conclude the terms of peace that he and Major Mishra had flown into Pakistan hours after the Prime Minister gave his commitment to attend. General Pratap had dismissed concerns over his personal safety in enemy territory: "A lion does not know the meaning of fear," he had said.

A hospital ward was now set up as an operations centre. An orderly summoned Major Mishra. The Pakistani Prime Minister stood amid intravenous drips, catheters and gauges. His expression was grim. He held a phone out to Major Mishra.

"They want to talk to you," he said. The national security advisor of India, Subrata Bose, was on the line.

"Mishra, what the hell is going on?"

Instinctively, Major Mishra clicked his heels to attention.

"Sir, General Pratap is ill. We are in the hospital. The doctors got to him just in time."

"What did those bastard Pakistanis do to him? You were there, tell me quickly what did they do?"

"Nothing as far as I could tell, sir."

"Mishra, are they threatening you to keep silent about this? Are they holding a gun to your head?"

"No, sir. We were sitting at the conference table—"

"We heard that story. Frankly, I don't believe it."

"It was shocking, sir."

"You're in on it, aren't you? You're in on whatever is going on."

"Sir?"

"What did they promise you, Mishra? Money? Girls?"

"Sir, I'm telling you the truth—"

"Whatever they offered you, we can do better. We have more money and much better girls—"

"Sir, I am not lying."

"You're saying Pratap just fell over at the conference table with a heart attack?"

"That's what happened, sir."

"Fool! We have Pratap's medical charts. Our best doctors have examined him for the last thirty years. He is fit. He was completely fit before he left for Pakistan."

"Then it is a mystery—"

"Mishra! Don't mistake me for an idiot. I know what's going on. How long have you been planning this with the Pakistanis? Do you know that I could have you court-martialled?"

"That's ridiculous!" Major Mishra blurted.

Subrata Bose took a breath and lowered his tone. His voice was full of menace. "Listen, Mishra. I don't know what your game is, but I'm going to find out. And when I do, you're going to be sorry. In the meantime, I want you to arrange to move General Pratap to the military plane and get him back here."

"Sir, the doctors say he can't be moved."

"Mishra, damn it, listen to me. I want him back in India. The flight to the closest Indian hospital is less than thirty minutes."

"Sir, they tell me that General Pratap will die if we move him out of intensive care."

"I don't care what they say! I want you to move him now!" The national security advisor was shouting so loudly that it made the Pakistani surveillance unit monitoring the conversation completely redundant.

Major Mishra spoke, his voice level: "Sir, I cannot follow your order. My first duty is to my general. I have sworn to protect his life."

The national security advisor began to hyperventilate. "Mishra–" he said finally. "If Pratap does not return to India – alive – you can tell your Pakistani friends that they can expect the war to continue. And now we won't be talking conventional war. Pratap is our national hero. If they kill him and think we will sit back and believe he died of natural causes, they are fools."

Subrata Bose hung up. Major Mishra began to relay the message to the Pakistanis, but was cut off.

"I heard," said the Pakistani Prime Minister. "Well, Mishra, what do we do?"

A cardiologist burst into the room. A stethoscope swung from his neck like a necklace. A nametag was sewn into his white doctor's coat. It read: Abdul Latif.

"He's fading."

"What are his chances?" the Prime Minister asked.

"Less than ten per cent. His heart has failed completely."

"Dying is not an option, doctor," snapped the Pakistani Prime Minister. "Your patient does not represent one life – thousands will die if he dies. Maybe millions."

The doctor shrugged. "I am not God."

"Is there anything we can do?"

The doctor looked around the room as if he was searching for inspiration.

"We could try a transplant, but it is risky. He might die during surgery."

"He's dying anyway," retorted the Prime Minister.

"We would have to find a proper match."

"Put out the word to every hospital in the country."

The doctor stubbornly gripped the ends of his stethoscope.

"We need to get consent from General Pratap's family. He could die during surgery."

Major Mishra spoke: "General Pratap's only family has been the Indian army. He is like my own brother. I give consent."

The doctor nodded and ran out of the room. The Prime Minister shook Major Mishra's hand. "You're doing the right thing."

Major Mishra unloosed his hand. He felt uneasy about this alliance. He levelled eyes with the Prime Minister:

"If word of this transplant gets to India—"

"It won't," said the Prime Minister. "I promise no one in India will ever find out."

Major Mishra nodded. The transplant would have to be kept secret: What patriotic Indian could accept that the bosom of India's most beloved son concealed a Pakistani heart?

*   *   *   *   *

General Pratap returned to India with the welcome befitting a hero. The official press releases announcing the secret talks did not mention the extra week he had spent in the Pakistani hospital. Neither was attention paid to the outcome of the negotiations. The few newspaper columnists who criticised General Pratap for yielding too much to the Pakistanis were dismissed as curmudgeons.

A welcome guard greeted the general in New Delhi. Major Mishra stayed close behind his commander. The public appearance was brief, for General Pratap was in considerable pain. The Pakistani cardiologist, Abdul Latif, had requested that General Pratap's private physician be informed of the transplant, but Major Mishra and the Pakistani Prime Minister vetoed the idea. Once the secret was out, there would be no containing it. The Indian government and General Pratap himself were told that the stitches on the patient's chest were the result of quadruple bypass surgery.

At a brief press conference, General Pratap was mobbed by reporters who asked for his impressions of the talks in Pakistan: "The soldier's foremost duty is to peace, not war," the General said. "I fought twice as hard for peace as I did in war."

Accounts of the interview said, "Pratap the lion-hearted has become Pratap the lion-hearted statesman." There were murmurings of a possible run for public office. But the hero was not heard from again for several months. The Indian doctors thought General Pratap took an unusually long time to recover from bypass surgery, but did not make their concerns public. Major Mishra nursed General Pratap day and night.

Every evening the first month, Major Mishra called Dr. Latif. The Indian briefed the Pakistani cardiologist about the patient: "He was quiet today," or "he was in some pain," or "the doctors are worried about infection setting in." As best he could, the doctor would assess the situation and prescribe medicines. Major Mishra would get the prescriptions filled.

After two months, Major Mishra and Dr Latif took to commending each other on the success of the "remote control" treatment.

"Hi Arjun, what news from the lion?" the cardiologist would ask.

"He's snoring, Abdul," Major Mishra would reply. "Can you prescribe anything for that?"

The doctor laughed. "He sounds fine. Maybe I should prescribe a sedative for you."

Major Mishra marvelled that no one had discovered he was making so many international calls to Pakistan. The state of Indian intelligence was clearly in a shambles, he reflected. He did not know that a surveillance truck had been stationed outside the army hospital where General Pratap was convalescing. For months now, Ranjit Malhotra, a top intelligence official, had been compiling a dossier. Transcripts of Major Mishra's conversations were regularly finding their way to the national security advisor.

*   *   *   *   *

As soon as General Pratap was able to sit up in bed, he began asking for books. He declined popular fiction. Instead, he developed an extensive reading list which included Mahatma Gandhi's autobiography, Albert Einstein's reflections on nuclear war and texts on Buddhism.

Major Mishra was taken aback at the choices, but put it down to lassitude induced by the long bed rest. Each morning, the officer strolled to a bookstore and ordered the latest item on the list. The clerks at the store soon greeted him familiarly and Major Mishra got to know some of the other regular patrons. As he stood in the checkout line, holding Confucius in one hand and Tolstoy in the other, he quickly adopted the habits and postures of a reader of refined taste: He glared disapprovingly at people buying the latest John Grisham novel or self-help book. As he strode out of the bookstore, he made sure that the impressive titles under his arm were clearly visible to passers-by. In this way, he made the work of the two intelligence agents shadowing him that much easier. Along with the transcripts of the phone calls to Pakistan, Ranjit Malhotra now placed the list of titles on the desk of the national security advisor.

General Pratap's face brightened each time Major Mishra brought him the latest offering. As he accepted the books, he would try to explain to his junior officer his line of thinking in ordering the books. "Mishra, have you ever considered the parallels between Gandhi and Confucius?" he would ask.

"No, sir," said Major Mishra truthfully.

"Hmm," the General mused. He folded his fingers into a steeple above his chest. "There is so much in the life of the prophets that is instructive, if we would only stop to listen. But we are too busy, making money, getting elected, fighting wars. I keep asking myself, why did our government just launch a war against Pakistan?"

"It was the Pakistanis who were the aggressors," said Major Mishra, bristling. "The Indian people demanded the war to defend their country. Any government that questioned this would get thrown out of office!"

"Yes," mused General Pratap with a twinkle in his eye. "Although sometimes I wonder if it is the other way around. The government demands the war to defend its office and any Indian people who question this get thrown out of the country?"

Major Mishra looked shocked and General Pratap laughed. "It was a joke," he said. "Only a joke."

Conversations such as this began to trouble Major Mishra. On his own initiative, he brought hardbound editions of Jane's *All the World's Fighting Ships* and biographies of military conquerors to the patient's room. On subsequent visits, he noticed that the General was using the military books as bookends to shore up the stack of non-violent and literary texts. Bringing the General boxes of fan mail from his admirers across the country proved similarly useless. General Pratap emptied the letters under his bed and used the boxes to store notes he was making from his scholarly readings.

After much hesitation, Major Mishra decided to confide

in the one person who might be able to shed some light on the matter. He delicately explained the situation to Dr. Abdul Latif. The Pakistani cardiologist said that the near-death experiences of some patients prompted them to re-evaluate their lives.

"But that won't explain the change in his personality, Abdul," said Major Mishra. "There's something wrong with him."

"Have you noticed hallucinations, delusions, anxiety?"

"No, the General seems happy and relaxed."

"So what you're saying is that you are unhappy with the change in his personality."

"It's just so unlike him. Excuse me for putting it this way, Abdul, but General Pratap has always hated Pakistanis."

"Hate is a corrosive emotion," replied the doctor. "We are healthier without it."

"So there's nothing that you can prescribe for him?"

"It seems to me that you are one with the problem."

* * * * *

It never occurred to Subrata Bose, the national security advisor, that Major Mishra was buying the books so that he or anyone else could read them. Subrata Bose prized the fact that his mind worked exclusively in the realm of espionage and foul play. It took him a few days to pierce the deception. The books were Major Mishra's ready-made cipher – according to some prearranged code, he was passing military secrets to the Pakistanis.

Towards the end of the fifth month after General Pratap's return to India, an aide to the national security advisor burst into his office one morning to say that the general had scheduled an impromptu press conference.

"Turn on the television," snapped Subrata Bose. "General Pratap knows all media appearances must be cleared through my office."

The first shock was that General Pratap was not dressed in his military uniform. Subrata Bose squinted unfamiliarly at the television. The General was wearing simple white cotton clothes. He was standing outside the military hospital – it was his first day of convalescence out of bed. The officials noted that General Pratap was not glaring into the camera, his eyes hooded, as had previously been his wont. He was smiling broadly, displaying a row of flawless teeth, and pressing his palms together.

"I want to thank you all for coming," General Pratap told the assembled reporters and television cameramen. "I know it was short notice, but sometimes the small voice of conscience demands to be heard immediately."

"What the hell?" said Subrata Bose.

"I wish to tell the Indian people that I am resigning from the military," General Pratap said. "Like other conquerors, including the famous King Ashok, I have decided to turn my attention to peace instead of war."

"It's Mishra," said Subrata Bose to himself. "It's that damn Major Mishra."

A reporter asked General Pratap why he had reached these conclusions now, after several decades in the military.

"The small voice of conscience – and I am using a phrase from Mahatma Gandhi here – works in mysterious ways," said General Pratap. "I don't have an appetite for war. I find that I no longer wish to fight my brothers."

Subrata Bose noticed that in the background, Major Mishra appeared to look guilty. A monstrous idea struck the national security advisor. The more he thought about it, the more plausible it became. He extracted the dossier that held the transcripts of the intercepted conversations between Major Mishra and the Pakistani cardiologist. He gazed at the unfamiliar names of the medicines that Dr. Abdul Latif had prescribed. Until this moment, Subrata Bose had assumed they were controlling General Pratap's pain and warding off infections.

"Get me the chief of cardiology at the All India Institute of Medical Sciences," said Subrata Bose to an aide. "And send a security detail to the hospital. Make sure no one enters and no one leaves for the next two hours. Especially not that damn Major Mishra. If he tries to make any more telephone calls, confiscate the phone and place him under arrest."

Subrata Bose peered over the transcripts again. A steely glint entered his eye. He had been a fool not to see through the deception. A short while later, there was a knock on the door and a white-coated doctor was ushered into the room.

"Dr. Anand," said Subrata Bose, rising to shake hands with the visitor. "Please sit down. I have called you here in a matter of the gravest national importance." Subrata Bose handed him the list of medicines that Dr Latif had prescribed. "Take a look at the names of these drugs, doctor. Can you deduce why they were prescribed?"

The doctor glanced at the list. His inspection was brief. "They are a list of antibiotics, heart medications and immune system suppressants," he replied. "I would say the most probable explanation is that they are being used to treat a patient who has had a transplant of some kind, maybe a heart transplant. The immune suppressants are to prevent the patient from rejecting the foreign organ."

Subrata Bose nodded. "Tell me doctor, can a patient with a heart transplant be moved from one intensive care unit to another hospital, transported in a plane, a few days after surgery?"

"It would be most inadvisable," said the cardiologist. "Anything can be done, of course, but there are so many complications. Besides, the patient would be in excruciating pain. May I ask who the patient is that you are speaking about?"

"One last thing, doctor," said the national security advisor, ignoring the question. "Do patients who have undergone a heart transplant ever report a change in personality?"

"No," said Dr. Anand with a smile. "The heart is a muscle like any other. It's the most important muscle in the body, but it plays no role in behaviour."

"Isn't the heart the seat of our emotions?"

"Only according to poets and writers. That is not science, it is a matter of literary license."

Subrata Bose regarded the cardiologist for a long moment.

"Doctor, there are some things that your science does not know."

*   *   *   *   *

Cell Number 44 had a long history of breaking the spirit of recalcitrant prisoners. Major Mishra almost brought that distinguished streak to an end, with his stubborn refusal to admit that he was the traitor who had helped engineer the Pakistani plan to subvert the Indian military. It was true that Major Mishra had been trained in the army to withstand the rigors of psychological and physical torture and it was also true that he happened to be a brave man. But his refusal to come clean after endless days of questioning and coercion struck his jailers as pathological.

He admitted to the heart transplant readily enough. Once he learned that the deception had been pierced, he switched gears and concocted a story about the circumstances surrounding it, about why he had been unwilling to let General Pratap or any other Indian learn about the operation.

"I was trying to avert war between India and Pakistan," he said.

"In that case, you should have followed my orders and moved General Pratap back to India," replied Subrata Bose.

"General Pratap would have died. The heart transplant was the only way to keep him alive – moving him to a plane and out of Pakistan would have killed him."

"And you know this as a result of your long years of training as a cardiologist?" the national security advisor asked sardonically.

"Abdul, that is Dr. Abdul Latif said the situation was critical."

"Even assuming this cock and bull story is true, what made you trust the word of a Pakistani doctor?"

"He was a doctor. He had no reason to lie."

"No reason to lie? You did not consider that he was part of the plan to steal the heart of our hero?"

"That's ridiculous."

Subrata Bose's eyes flashed. "I'll have you know your plan has failed, Mishra," he said. "General Pratap is currently on the operating table. He is undergoing surgery. We're retransplanting his heart – this time with a patriotic Indian organ."

"You're mad," cried Major Mishra.

Subrata Bose angrily gestured to the jailers and they tightened the bolt that ran behind the prisoner's back. Major Mishra's left shoulder was detached from its socket. It made a pop that sounded like the cork of a champagne bottle being opened. It took several minutes for the prisoner's cries to abate.

"Tell me about the books," said Subrata Bose.

Major Mishra looked haggard. He slumped forward in his chair, suspended only by the scaffolding that had been erected around him. He looked like an abandoned building that had been stripped of its interiors in preparation for the wrecking crew. Grime and stubble and sweat and blood were caked in an unholy mess on his face, and his limbs were twisted into fantastical angles. If he tried to answer the question, the sounds emanating from his mouth were indistinguishable from incoherent moans. Saliva dripped from his lips. It was clear he no longer had the power to close his own mouth.

The national security advisor stood behind his prisoner with one hand over his heart. When he spoke, it seemed he addressed not the tattered form beside him, but was soliloquising to some imaginary audience.

"Even if everything you say is true," he said, "did it not occur to you that when General Pratap began reading Mahatma Gandhi's autobiography that something was seriously wrong?"

There was no answer. With a sad shake of his head, Subrata Bose left the room. The jailers completed the formalities. A signed confession was obtained from the prisoner. The signature on the sheet was legible because the jailers were professionals – like skilled surgeons, they had taken care to save the fingers of Major Mishra's right hand.

The Ghosts of Kashmir

I

Madan Singh watched the shadow of the army jeep elongate as the pale sun swung down over Dal Lake. Soldiers went back and forth from the jeep to an enclosure fortified by sandbags. Sentries peered over machine gun barrels as people walked by huddled in pherans and shawls. No one levelled eyes with the soldiers. The fog arrived, swirling around the dome of the Hazratbal mosque, erasing its graceful contours. Through a gap in the window, the wind whistled. Madan shivered.

"Where is the lawyer?" a voice asked.

Madan looked up startled. He had heard neither knock nor footstep. A hunched old man in tattered, musty clothes stood at the door. He was coughing into a handkerchief. Having arrived only a week before, Madan knew the man wanted his mentor, Ghulam Mohammed. "He's away at the High Court. Can I help you?"

The visitor bent over in another spasm of coughing. He looked as it he was in his seventies, with fading hair and a patchy beard flecked with white. As he gasped for breath, Madan remembered his mentor's advice to use the early moments of an interview to size up a client. Ghulam Mohammed said good lawyers could figure out what their clients wanted before they had uttered a single word. People's troubles and secrets, he had declared, were like their medical ailments, jealously guarded but visible to the trained eye. Did they seem aggrieved or anxious? Did they seem in a rush to acquire legal representation? Did they post a bodyguard at the door – a sign that criminal connections were probably involved?

"I need a lawyer," the old man finally said. His voice was raspy, as if from disuse. "My Basheer, my son has – are you a lawyer?"

"I am," Madan said crisply, waving at a recently framed certificate on the wall. *The National Law School of India, Bangalore, hereby attests that Mandan Doha Singh has completed all requirements towards the degree Bachelor of Laws.* Madan had hung a flowering plant to hide the date on the bottom of the certificate because it was only weeks old. Before the visitor could discover his inexperience, Madan led him to a chair. He himself sat behind Ghulam Mohammed's desk, and folded his fingers into a pyramid in the manner of his mentor.

"Please tell me why you have come?" he asked, trying with his tone to convey both firmness and solicitude.

"My son has been charged – they said Section 38, but I'm not sure. They are going to torture him. Please, please do something! He is a good boy. Harmless. My only child. My wife and I are old and what will we do without our Basheer? Look, here is his picture."

"This is your son?" the lawyer asked, surprised. The photograph showed a man who was not much older than Madan himself. The picture had been taken in a studio with a blue background, and the young man's face was turned at a slight angle. His hair was moulded into a glamorous wave and a small smile played on his lips.

"That is Basheer," the man confirmed, his eyes brimming.

"Did I tell you he was a poet? A very fine poet. His couplets were famous for miles around. He fell in with a bad crowd. What to do, that is the way things are these days. You will help us, won't you?"

"How long has it been since your son was taken into custody?"

"Eight years."

"Eight years! I thought this was a new case."

"For his mother and I, eight years and eight minutes is the same thing. Not an hour passes, not a second in an hour, when we are not thinking of Basheer. For a parent," he sighed, "urgency can't be measured in time, it must be measured in love."

He seemed much more eloquent in describing his feelings for his son than in describing the case, Madan thought. Was that the norm for all fathers and all cases?

"Basheer once wrote something like that in his poems," the man continued. "I carry it everywhere. Will you give it to him when you see him? He'll know I still remember the days we used to exchange poetry."

He handed Madan a page torn out of a notebook. The page had a number of handwritten couplets. The first read:

Lovers do not wear watches, they cannot tell time

Love's seconds are measured only by the beating of hearts.

"I don't know what the case is about," Madan said, turning the photo around in one hand and the page of couplets in the other. "What are the charges against him?"

The father coughed painfully again and said: "The usual, sir. Everyone is charged with such things these days. Some get away scot-free, but they imprisoned my Basheer."

The man pushed forward an envelope with papers. The lawyer briefly inspected them; they were photocopies of briefs filed by other lawyers. A yellowing document near the top was addressed to a local judge and made the argument that twenty year-old Basheer Ahmed was not a Pakistan-trained terrorist, that he had not blown up an army barracks, and that he had not been involved in a shootout that killed several Indian soldiers. Madan could not find documents that laid out the prosecution's charges.

"Is this lawyer no longer representing your son?" he asked.

"We have been to so many lawyers that I have stopped counting."

"Where is your son being held?"

The man pointed to the top of the envelope where an address had been scrawled in red ink.

"When was the last time you saw your son?" Madan asked.

"The security forces took him away eight years ago. But he fell in with bad company even earlier. He would come home late at night and slip out before dawn. He stopped showing me his poems, and that was how I knew."

"So the last time you saw him was eight years ago, right before he was arrested?" Madan wanted to cut through the father's emotional tangles and get to the facts.

The old man looked down at his feet, pursing his lips.

"Well?" Madan said. "I cannot help you if you don't tell me the truth."

"Eight summers ago, sir, that is eight years ago–" he began hesitantly.

"Yes?"

"They told me Basheer had been killed."

"Killed!"

"Lies, sir. They were lying." The father clasped his hands. "They were holding him in secret without trial."

"How do you know that?" Madan asked. "Did you see your son again?"

"He came to me every day—" he choked and covered his mouth with the handkerchief, trying to stifle the coughs racking his body – "every day in my dreams, that first year."

"I mean in real life," said Madan, irritated by the visitor's ramblings. "Did you actually *see* your son after he was taken away?"

"Yes," he replied softly. "Seven years ago, I was very ill and they relented and allowed my Basheer to spend a night with me. They thought I was going to die and they took pity on an old man."

"Have you seen him since then?"

"I am not allowed to visit him. And I am mostly confined to my bed because of my sickness." He showed the handkerchief to Madan. The lawyer drew back sharply. The cloth was splattered with blood. Madan gathered together the legal papers, the couplets, and the photograph of Basheer Ahmed, and placed them in a new file.

The old man leaped to his feet. "I can't give that to you."

The lawyer was astouaded. "You can't give me the legal papers?"

"The photograph."

"I'd like to keep it temporarily, for purposes of identification and evidence—"

"No!" He lunged forward, veins protruding from of his neck, his fingers bunched into fists.

"I will take care not to misplace it," said Madan, hurriedly.

"Give it back."

The lawyer detached the photograph and handed it back. Ghulam Mohammed had warned him that clients could be difficult. They could be emotional and unpredictable – this was probably what he had meant. Good lawyers never took their clients' problems personally, Ghulam Mohammed had said on Madan's first day in Srinagar, and the young lawyer realised the value of that advice.

He put the photograph carefully in his pocket. "Thank you for helping an old man," he said gently. He laid a business card on the table. It read: *Shakeel Ahmed, Photo Studio* and gave an address in the old part of the city.

"Will you give the couplets to my son?"

"It is not professional for lawyers to transfer personal

effects to a prisoner," replied Madan, "but perhaps I will make an exception just this once."

"You have the eternal gratitude of a father," the man said, raising one hand in salute. He slipped out of the office as silently as he had arrived.

Madan sat back and thought about the picture of Shakeel Ahmed's son. The photograph of Basheer Ahmed had probably been taken in his father's studio. The old man had probably taken the picture himself. Why else would he be so sentimental about such an idealised image?

Madan wondered whether he should wait for Ghulam Mohammed to return before starting on the case. What if his mentor steered him away from it? Besides the vagueness of the case, the father had made no mention of payment. It seemed unlikely he could afford very much. Ghulam Mohammed would probably turn down the case. Madan flipped through the papers and came across another of Basheer Ahmed's couplets:

Lovers are never punctual, lovers are never late

Tomorrow and yesterday mean nothing for the one in love.

Something about the case reminded Madan of a family he had grown close to in Bangalore, a Muslim sweetshop owner and his wife and their college-going son. The family had got mixed up with the wrong people and the wife had been assaulted during a time of communal tension. Madan, who was friendly with the woman, irrationally blamed himself. He knew the circumstances of Shakeel Ahmed and his wife and son were completely different. Kashmir was a different place. But something in him had been hollowed out by the episode, which had cost him a dear friendship and left him lonely. Joining a law practice in Kashmir was part of his effort to make amends. Fate had put this family in his hands and, both as a lawyer and as a human being, he wanted to help.

II

The Kashmir that Madan came to was a distant reflection of the Kashmir he had read about in books and seen in films. This was no idyllic tourist destination, but a brutal place of guns and barbed wire. Suspicion and fear were common currency and the unending war had drained the place of joy. As Madan stepped out of the office, he shivered again. The fog was dense and people on the streets seemed like wraiths; buildings and bridges faded in and out like mirages.

The address that Shakeel Ahmed had given him was at the edge of town, in an area that had once hosted an army barracks. After the soldiers were moved to a more secure location, the old site had fallen into disrepair. The autorickshaw dropped him off at a building at one end of the barracks. It looked more like an abandoned house than a detention facility for dangerous terrorists. It seemed a part of the shrubbery that grew wild around it. The walls were caked with moss and dirt. The main entrance was no longer visible. No windows were apparent, save two dark holes that balefully regarded the street like sightless eyes. Madan pushed at the gate tentatively. He found himself in a garden overgrown with weeds and creepers. An air of disuse hung about the place.

There was an opening without a door on the side of the building and it gave onto a narrow corridor. Framed portraits had once hung on the walls, for rectangular ridges were evident beneath the accumulating dust, and each missing frame boasted a rusting nail above it, like an exclamation mark. Madan wondered what pictures had hung in the corridor and when and why they had been removed. A gust of wind whipped through the corridor. Why was this ramshackle house a holding place for inmates awaiting trial? Where were the guards?

A door barred his way. The lawyer knocked. The wood was so heavy that he could barely hear the sound of his own knuckles. He knocked harder and then pounded on the door. It swung open suddenly.

"What do you want?" a voice barked.

It was dark inside. Madan dimly made out a sentry. He explained he had come to see a client. He could now make out the soldier's weather - beaten face. The man's uniform was crumpled. Madan was acutely conscious of his new suit, gleaming shoes and brand new briefcase. He realized he probably looked exactly like a lawyer out on his first case. He wished he had dressed more casually. The sentry motioned him to enter. Madan found himself in a cavernous room. There was a desk in the middle of the hall with a kerosene lamp. A hunched figure sat behind it. There were no electric lights. The two holes in the wall that the lawyer had spotted outside admitted faint twilight. What kind of detention facility was this? Madan tried to appear nonchalant as he walked towards the man who was dressed in civilian clothes. The desk was clear of stationery, telephones and office equipment. It was covered by a thick layer of dust.

"I'm here to see Basheer Ahmed," Madan said brusquely. "He's my client." When the man did not respond, Madan added, a little too loudly, "I am his lawyer."

The man's lips moved silently as if he was experimenting with them. When he spoke, it was in a hoarse voice so low that the lawyer had to lean forward to hear.

"Did the boy's father send you?"

"He offered me the case, yes."

"There have been others."

"He did mention other lawyers have been involved. The courts have dragged their feet."

"There are no court proceedings."

"Is he being held without trial? Justice delayed is justice denied, you know."

. The man looked at Madan like a teacher dealing with an exceedingly slow child. "It is good that the father cares so much about his son. The last time he sent a doctor."

"Why, what was wrong with Basheer Ahmed?"

"The doctor concluded Basheer was insane." The man's lips stretched slightly. In the light of the kerosene lamp, his cheeks had the texture of old leather. "In fact, the doctor concluded we were all insane."

Madan blinked. "Do you mean he's mad?"

"One man's madness is another's sanity."

Madan felt a hot flush rise to his cheeks. The collar tag on his new coat tickled the inside of his neck. "I want to see my client," he said sharply. "He's a prisoner and entitled to legal representation. It is my duty to investigate. There may be another facility where he might be more comfortable. And better cared for."

The old man was not provoked. "As the warden here, I can tell you that no one ever leaves."

Bureaucrats made the worst jailers, Madan thought, because they could not imagine a world where things were different. The two men stared at each other. The lawyer refused to yield ground.

"Very well," the warden said. "I will let you see him. It will probably do him good."

He rummaged under the desk and produced a ring the size of a child's bicycle wheel. Dozens of keys hung from it. He held out the keys: "Go down that flight of stairs, and then turn right. He is in the last cell. Take the lamp with you."

Madan was stunned at how cavalier the wizened old man was about security. He tried to stay impassive as he picked up the kerosene lamp. As he stepped away from the desk, the ring of keys reminded Madan of the myth of the demon who threaded his victims' thumbs into a giant garland. Each key was like a finger – each key a life. A door at the side of the hall yielded to a narrow set of stairs. It was pitch dark, so Madan held the lamp high and felt for the edge of each step with the tips of his shoes. He emerged in the middle of another long corridor. Dark cells fell off on either side and, at the sound of the lawyer, inmates pushed up against the bars like bored animals. Some rattled the bars, others called out to him. The kerosene lamp cast gloomy shadows over the prisoner's faces. The young lawyer was not sure what hardened criminals looked like, but the men in the cells did not belong to such a category.

Their eyes were haggard and bloodshot, their faces gnarled. Age and time hung over the cells like dense cobwebs. The hands that gripped the bars showed skin like translucent parchment stretched over knuckles and tendons. The prisoners had hollow cheeks and prominent temples. They looked like walking x-ray images. Their prison garb was so soiled that its original colours were indeterminable. Had madness caused the men to be imprisoned or the other way around? Who could remain sane in such a place?

The kerosene lamp threw ten foot-shadows of the prisoners on the walls, and the dark shapes hovered on either side of Madan as he walked to Basheer Ahmed's cell. He grit his teeth and suppressed an urge to run out of the place. Prisoners called out to him as he passed. Some reached out and tried to touch his shoes. They shouted curses, slogans and pleas. The collective wailing made the hairs on the back of his neck stand on end. One of the cells at the end of the corridor appeared empty. He turned his attention to the other. A man stood at the bars. His face was bloodstained.

"Hello," Madan said tentatively, trying not to sound shocked. "My name is Madan Singh. Your father—"

The man proffered a hand through the bars for a handshake. Madan hesitated.

The man's lips moved inarticulately. Then, croaking like the warden, "Chawla," he said. "I am Captain Vikram Chawla of the Border Security Force."

An Indian officer imprisoned here along with suspected militants and terrorists — was he a deserter or a spy? "I'm sorry," Madan said, moving back. "I'm looking for Basheer Ahmed."

"Swine!" Chawla screamed, violently rattling the bars. "Basheer Ahmed, the swine. I killed him with my own two hands—"

"Over here," called out a voice. Madan whirled. The voice came from the opposite cell, the one he had thought was empty.

"I am Basheer Ahmed," said the voice.

The soldier continued to scream obscenities. Madan turned away with a hurried apology. Maybe the doctor was right, everyone here was mad.

No one stood at the bars of Basheer Ahmed's cell. Madan had to strain to make out a metal chair bolted to the far wall. A man sat in the chair with restraints around his wrists and ankles. Like the other prisoners, Basheer Ahmed looked emaciated. Madan felt uneasy. He wondered about the prudence of entering the cell of a dangerous terrorist, but seeing that Basheer Ahmed could not move, he inserted keys into the padlock until he found the one that produced a series of clicks. Glistening strands of spider webs stretched as the cell door opened.

Wisps of beard and moustache hung from Basheer Ahmed's face. Deep wrinkles on his forehead made him look twice his age. The chains about him were drawn so tight that the lawyer wondered how the inmate could urinate or feed himself. If the bars had not been opened in a long while, did that mean the prisoner was fed where he sat, by a long spoon? Madan Singh shook his head. The questions would have to wait.

There was a small concrete ledge in the cell, which could have served as a hard bed. Madan sat down gingerly on it.

Basheer Ahmed stared at him without blinking. Madan fished out the scrap of paper with the couplets and held it up by way of introduction. "Do you recognise these poems? My name is Madan Singh. I'm a lawyer. Your father has asked me to take on your case. He wanted me to give this to you."

Madan dropped the page of couplets in the prisoner's lap. Basheer Ahmed peered down at them. When he looked up, there were tears in his eyes.

"Thank you for bringing it," he said.

"You're welcome."

"It has been so many years since I saw this page. Isn't it strange? I once thought I was going to be a poet."

"There's still time for that. You have many years remaining for art."

"The time for that has passed," the prisoner said quietly.

"Your father said your poems were well known. Do you still write poetry?"

Basheer Ahmed nodded. "It is difficult to find an audience for them. I wrote mainly for my father. He was my favourite reader. He rarely gets to read my poems now."

Madan wondered how Basheer Ahmed could write poems while he was restrained in this manner. "He told me it has been seven years since you saw him."

"The doctors said he was dying."

"What was he suffering from?"

"Tuberculosis."

Madan remembered Shakeel Ahmed's bloodstained handkerchief. "He also told me he dreamed of you many times the year after you were brought here."

"I was able to visit him then, yes."

Madan weighed the strange comment. A doctor had once told him it was pointless to contradict delusional people. He decided to take another tack. He asked gently, "Basheer, do you know why your father asked me to take your case?"

Basheer Ahmed looked down at the couplets. "To give these to me."

"That is not the reason I came to see you," Madan said. "This is only poetry, a gift from your father. It has no bearing on your case. Do you understand me, Basheer? You are in a detention facility for the criminally insane. You have been charged with terrorism. Perhaps we should talk about your case?"

"We are talking about my case."

"From a legal perspective, I mean. Have you had a court hearing?"

Basheer Ahmed shook his head.

"Your father gave me a number of briefs filed by other lawyers."

"Do you know the charges against me?"

"I could not find the official document."

"I hurt my parents terribly," said Basheer Ahmed. "I stole from them, lied. I used people, a girl who loved me–"

"What are the legal charges?" Madan interrupted.

"It was a shoot-out," Basheer Ahmed replied quietly. "I have often relived that night. There were seven of us in the attic of a house. The security forces found our location and surrounded us. There was a gun-battle and all six of my comrades were killed. We killed many soldiers, too. In the end, it came down to Chawla and myself."

"Chawla? The man in the opposite cell!"

"He had been pursuing me since I helped to blow up an army barracks," said Basheer Ahmed. "By the time he came into the attic, neither of us had ammunition. He had a knife. I knew what he would do if he captured me. One of my comrades had dropped a hand grenade on the floor. I held it up and pulled the pin. I warned Chawla we would both die. I told him to run. But he just stood there."

"I don't understand," said Madan. "Did it not explode?"

"Yes, it did."

Madan sat back against the wall. He regarded Basheer Ahmed with a mixture of apprehension and sympathy. "I cannot help you," he said shortly. "You do not need a lawyer, you need a psychiatrist."

Basheer Ahmed's tone changed. "I'm sorry if I have offended you."

Madan shrugged. "You don't have to worry about my feelings. Lawyers don't take their clients' problems personally."

The prisoner regarded Madan sadly. "The only reason my father came to you is because he knew you would take our case personally."

"What are you talking about?" Madan asked sharply.

The prisoner averted his eyes. "You seem like a kind man, a new lawyer. We need intermediaries like you in order to communicate."

Madan thought about Shakeel Ahmed and the photocopied legal briefs, the glossy, sentimental photograph, the warden, the unkempt sentry, this decrepit detention facility. And here was Basheer Ahmed chained in his cell across from the soldier who had pursued him for years. Madan felt paralysed.

"Please don't be afraid," the prisoner said. "I want you to take something from my pocket and pass it on to my parents."

The nape of the lawyer's neck prickled.

"Did they tell you I was dangerous?" Basheer Ahmed whispered.

Madan wanted to run.

"It's right here, in my shirt pocket," the prisoner pleaded. When Madan did not move, he repeated, "please don't be afraid."

Madan crept towards the chained figure and quickly dug into Basheer Ahmed's pocket. It felt like he was reaching through the prisoner's ribs, into his heart. His fingers found a tightly folded wad of paper. He grabbed it and jumped back. Basheer Ahmed did not move. Madan looked down at his hand.

"More poems?" he asked, incredulous.

"Yes," said Basheer Ahmed. "And something else. I meant to return it to my mother a long time ago."

The folded paper concealed something metallic. At first, Madan thought it was a bullet, but when he unfolded the sheet of paper, he found an antique gold ring embedded with diamonds. "It is not professional for lawyers to transfer personal effects between prisoners and their families," Madan stammered. "I'm not sure when I'll see your father again."

"It would mean so much to them," the prisoner replied. "Didn't my father give you an address?"

Madan recalled that Shakeel Ahmed had left a business card. Keeping his eyes on Basheer Ahmed, he backed away, holding the folded paper, the kerosene lamp and the keys.

The prisoner whispered, "My family is forever in your debt."

Madan stepped outside the cell and locked it. As he made his way up the corridor, the voices from the other cells started up again, more fervently than before. Some of the prisoners hurled themselves at the bars and rattled them violently. Madan began to run. The voices pursued him. He stumbled on the stairs and fell, dropping the kerosene lamp. He scrambled up and burst into the hall. It was pitch black. No light came from the holes in the wall. Where had the warden gone? Madan dropped the keys and felt blindly for the door, trying desperately to remember the layout of the hall. He found the door, threw it open and stumbled into the narrow corridor.

Night had fallen. He ran into the garden, feeling thorns

and brambles rip at his trousers. He did not stop until he was outside the gate. From the street, the building was almost invisible against the darkness. Madan could no longer hear the screams.

III

He was very tired, but he did not walk homeward. His steps carried him towards the old part of the city, where the streets wound around each other like entwined lovers. He shivered every few steps, as he remembered the screams. He asked himself why he was walking towards the old city, when he should have been going home, to a warm blanket and a hot cup of tea.

He stopped at a roadside teashop and asked the vendor the way to the address printed on Shakeel Ahmed's business card. The man pointed down one street. Madan walked on. He had some difficulty finding the studio for it was concealed among larger houses. There was a street lamp down the block that flickered on and off, as if it could not make up its mind. In the flashes of light, Madan made out the small, dilapidated sign for the studio. No light shone through the windows. There was no doorbell. The lawyer wondered whether to knock. The door was old and looked as if it might come off its hinges if he banged too hard. He called out Shakeel Ahmed's name a few times.

The door opened a crack. Madan could not tell who stood behind the door.

"Who is it?" asked a woman's thin voice.

"I'm a lawyer," Madan said, unsure of what to say. "Your

husband, that is Mr. Shakeel Ahmed, asked me today to take on your son's case."

For a few moments, the lawyer heard nothing.

"You saw Basheer?" the voice finally asked.

"I just returned from –" the lawyer hesitated. "From the detention facility."

"You saw Basheer?" she asked again.

"Yes. I spent some time with your son."

"Come inside."

The door opened. Inside, a small oil lamp threw a soft glow over a table and a few chairs. Madan peered around. Portraits hung on the walls. The light was too dim to make out the details. Basheer Ahmed's mother guided him to a chair.

"How is he?" she asked.

"He seems all right," he replied, wondering how much she already knew. Should he mention that Basheer Ahmed was manacled? Wouldn't previous messengers have conveyed this already? Or would they have had the same reluctance to break bad news to a parent? The table was dusty and Madan removed his elbow from it in the interest of his new suit. The old lady sat down on another chair. A shawl was wrapped over her head and partially fell across her face like a veil. She held the shawl at her throat with bony fingers. She was a small woman, and her hunched posture made her seem even smaller.

"How much time did you spend with him?" she asked.

"It might have been fifteen minutes."

"Is he still bound to a chair?"

"Yes," he said, grateful that she knew. To make her feel better, he added, "He did not seem uncomfortable."

"Everyone adjusts to their circumstances," she said. "What use would it be to feel uncomfortable?"

Madan nodded awkwardly. "He thinks of you frequently. He seems to have warm memories."

"Yes," she said sadly. "That's all we have."

"His father asked me to give him some poetry. Basheer, that is Basheer Ahmed, seemed pleased to read them."

The old woman's eyes crinkled with pleasure.

"He also asked me to give you something."

The lawyer placed Basheer Ahmed's gift on the table. The mother unfolded it. The ring rolled onto the table, making a narrow track on the dusty surface. The diamonds glinted in the light of the lamp. She seized the ring. Almost immediately, she began to weep. Madan looked away. Clutching the ring to her heart, she cried silently into her shawl, her frail body shaking. The shawl came loose and the lawyer caught a glimpse of her features and saw the resemblance to Basheer Ahmed. He wondered what stories the ring contained, what memories it brought back. The strands that tied parent to child were as tangled as the streets he had recently walked. Sorrow, joy and hurt, nostalgia and regret met at intersections and went off their own ways and the memory of all those emotions was multiplied by the many years apart. The lawyer remembered how attached Shakeel Ahmed had been to the photograph of his son, a photograph that bore absurdly little resemblance to the real Basheer Ahmed. This was the consequence of love, Madan thought, for the eyes of love are sightless and cannot see the world as it truly is.

The lawyer tapped the sheet of poetry on the table.

"Is Shakeel Ahmed home?" he asked softly.

"He is not here," she said. "I have not seen my husband for seven years."

The numbers and dates swirled in Madan's head. He felt dizzy.

"Don't worry," she said. "He will come to see you again."

She pushed the sheet of poetry that Basheer Ahmed had given him across the table. "You had better give this to Basheer's father. I was never one for poetry." She reached into the folds of her dress and brought out a photograph. She placed it alongside the poems. "Would you be so kind as to give him this as well?" Madan took both items. Using the table for support, he got to his feet.

"I cannot tell you how grateful we are to you," she whispered.

Madan staggered out. His feet carried him to the street lamp, which was still flickering. In the flashes of light, the lawyer examined the photograph and the poems that he was to deliver to Shakeel Ahmed. The picture had been taken outdoors. It showed a man, woman and a child. They all looked incredibly young. The photograph concealed what time had done to the faces. Shakeel Ahmed and his wife wore jaunty smiles that were ignorant of tragedy. Both had an arm around the boy. Basheer Ahmed grinned boldly, with the confidence of a child who is utterly loved. It was an impossibly happy photograph, and knowing what he knew now, sadness welled up in the young lawyer's heart. He bit his lip to hold back tears. He opened the sheet of poems that Basheer Ahmed had given him. There were several couplets. The last two read:

> *Guns are not religious, bombs have no patriotism,*
> *The bullet in the man's skull does not understand his thoughts.*

> *The graveyards ask, "Who are the living, but the dead in waiting?"*
> *The ghosts reply, "Who are the dead, but the living in decay?"*

Madan put the sheet of paper and the photograph in his pocket. He walked on. The street lamp flickered for a few moments and then went out, like a coded message from another world.

Fear In The Valley
Non-Fiction

Gonipura Village, Northern Kashmir – At 1:20 in the afternoon on October 21, 2003, a white sport utility vehicle with the license plate number JK 050490 pulled onto the rutted streets of Gonipura village. Two men alighted and approached Haider Ahmed Bhat, a 25-year-old Muslim shopkeeper. According to eye-witnesses in the village, one man asked to buy cigarettes. As Bhat was completing the transaction, the second man seized the shopkeeper by the nape of his neck and shoved him into the vehicle. The two assailants leaped in after their victim and the vehicle sped away. Bhat's uncle, Ghulam Rasool Bhat, who witnessed the event, said there were two other men inside the vehicle who wore the uniforms of Indian army troops. Two weeks after the abduction, the shopkeeper's family was summoned to a police station in a remote area close to the Indian border with Pakistan. The family was asked by the police to identify the body of a militant killed during a shootout with the Indian army. The dead man was Haider Ahmed Bhat and he was badly disfigured, with bullet wounds behind his left ear, on his chest and his right shoulder, according to relatives and neighbours. The corpse was brought back to Gonipura for the funeral, and hundreds of mourners were still milling in a central courtyard when I visited the village the following day. The dead man's father, Mohammed Ahsan Bhat, told me his son had no links with militants; the villagers were certain that Bhat had been murdered in cold blood by the army and that troops had faked an encounter to dispose of the body. India's Ministry of Defence spokesman Mukhtiar Singh said, "there is no truth in this story," and asserted that the men who picked up Bhat from Gonipura were not army personnel. The uniforms worn by two of the abductors meant nothing, he said, since militants often disguised themselves in army fatigues. Security forces first encountered Bhat during the shootout, Singh said, adding, "one of our boys was injured" in the shootout. Singh called Haider Ahmed Bhat a "terrorist."

The abduction and killing went largely unnoticed: World media attention was not focused on Kashmir, and the Indian media seem to have imposed something of a blackout on troubles in this northern state, not because of censorship but audience fatigue. Since the late 1980s, a vicious insurgency fuelled by militants entering Kashmir from Pakistan has prompted India to maintain upto 750,000 soldiers, border guards and police to pacify the restive state. The conflict has centred in the beautiful Kashmir valley, a jagged oval about 90 miles in length. Between 40,000 and 100,000 people have been killed – official estimates vary greatly from civilian and separatist groups – and the half a dozen deaths that occur here on any given day are no longer considered newsworthy. Many Indian newspapers, however, regularly focus on how Pakistan has armed militants and embarrassed India by bringing up the Kashmir dispute at international fora; a flood of op-eds regularly analyse who is winning the intricate game of one-upmanship that is the obsession of both countries. Kashmir's significance in South Asia is unfortunately measured in terms of this zero sum game. Although both India and Pakistan claim to champion the cause of ordinary Kashmiris – and recent peace initiatives between the rivals have been heralded as a harbinger of better times – every single person I interviewed in Kashmir said neither India nor Pakistan represented the aspirations of Kashmiris.

Mohammed Ashraf, a neighbour of Haider Ahmed Bhat in Gonipura, said simply, "we have become scapegoats between India and Pakistan."

*   *   *   *   *

South Asia stepped back from the brink of war in 2002. The following year, India and Pakistan launched a "peace offensive" and opened talks about the future of Kashmir. The effort was praised in Washington and around the world. New Delhi also opened talks with the All Party Hurriyat Conference, a confederation of political parties in Kashmir whose members have aims ranging from increased autonomy to independence. For over a decade, India has accused Pakistan of infiltrating militants into Kashmir, often under cover of fire from Pakistani army positions. After the September 11 attacks, the Bush administration pressured Pakistan into ending its support for Kashmiri separatists. Pakistan maintains it offers the groups only diplomatic and "moral" support. It is unclear whether India's new Prime Minister Manmohan Singh, an economist with the Congress Party, can push forward the peace initiative launched by the previous Hindu nationalist government – indeed, it is not clear what there is to push forward. As I write these words in the summer of 2005, hundreds of people in Kashmir have been killed, wounded and abducted during the last months.

One Indian air force officer who served in Kashmir told me that after militants enter the homes of Kashmiris, Indian security forces cordon off the streets. After trying to get civilians out, the officer said, "we have to blow up the building – and that's when you get collateral damage." The officer, whom I met on a train from Delhi, declined to give his name. He held out little optimism for the peace initiative because no political party in India could afford to look weak on Kashmir. Ordinary Indians and Pakistanis want peace, he said, but the politicians would never allow it. This widespread theory is both heartening and disingenuous: There is a real and growing constituency for peace in South Asia. But for a growing number of Indians and Pakistanis, Kashmir has also become a litmus test of patriotism. To see the conflict from the point of view of Kashmiris would undermine each side's strategy in the zero sum game.

My plane from Delhi stopped in Jammu, the relatively calm winter capital of the state, where Hindus are in a majority. Still, as the plane landed at the airport, I saw army trucks stationed at either side of the runway and soldiers with rifles standing behind shoulder-high sandbags. About 200 people boarded the flight to Kashmir, but nearly everyone deplaned at Jammu. The empty plane flew on to the summer capital of Srinagar, which is in the heart of the valley of Kashmir. Seven soldiers armed with carbines and automatic weapons were waiting on the runway as I climbed off the plane, and dozens more were at the terminal. The road leading out of the airport had a series of fortifications, with soldiers stationed behind bunkers, sandbags and checkpoints. An interlaced structure of barricades forced taxis to weave back and forth across the road; my driver, Abdul Majid, accomplished this at greater speed than I thought possible – his car had the advantage of missing side-view mirrors. Majid told me the economy was in a shambles and unemployment was high. I was his first fare in 20 days. "India wants this land and Pakistan wants this land, too," he said in Hindi. "No one asks what we want."

* * * * *

Kashmir was ruled by King Hari Singh when India was partitioned by the British in August 1947. Both India and Pakistan claimed Kashmir, a Muslim majority state ruled by Singh, a Hindu. Two months later, tribals from Pakistan backed by the incipient Pakistani army invaded Kashmir. Singh appealed to India for help. New Delhi conditioned its support on Singh signing an Instrument of Accession which would give Kashmir to India; as soon as the document was signed, the Indian army fought a brief war with Pakistan and occupied two thirds of the state. Pakistan claimed the northern third. The line of control immediately became the subject of semantics. Pakistan called its territory Azad Kashmir meaning Free Kashmir. India referred to the same area as Pakistan Occupied Kashmir. At the United Nations, India agreed to hold a plebiscite for Kashmiris and Pakistan agreed to create the peaceful conditions necessary for such a poll; both countries have ever since accused the other of reneging on their word. As a schoolboy in India, maps in my geography textbooks always showed the third of Kashmir under Pakistani control as Indian territory – geographically, it was India's crown. I was outraged by atlases published by international mapmakers because they always showed my country with its crown knocked off. Today, mirroring the positions of their respective governments, Indian newspapers regularly describe atrocities in Pakistan-administered Kashmir while Pakistani newspapers focus on human rights abuses in Indian-administered Kashmir.

Similar narratives drive diplomacy: Pakistan, insecure about its much larger rival, seeks to show the countries are equals. During the early stage of the 2003 peace initiative, the Indian government offered to treat twenty Pakistani children at Indian hospitals. Pakistan responded by offering to treat forty

Indian children at Pakistani hospitals. If Pakistan suffers from an inferiority complex, India may have the opposite problem: If the United States could go after terrorists in Afghanistan after the September 11 attacks, several Indian strategists reasoned in 2002, why couldn't Indian troops invade Pakistan and dismantle militant training camps? Such rhetoric quickly causes tempers to flare in nuclear-armed South Asia: Pakistan's President Pervez Musharraf sternly warned, "neither are we Afghanistan nor should India think it is the United States." Ideologues in India and Pakistan regularly use Kashmir to their own ends: Most Indians know about the thousands of Hindus who were driven from their homes in Kashmir by a campaign of terror and now live in refugee camps. The plight of these Hindus is real, but their cause is inexplicably used to turn a blind eye toward the plight of millions of Kashmiri Muslims. Fundamentalists in Pakistan have similarly painted the plight of Kashmiris as part of an international siege against Muslims, although the roots of the conflict here and the culture of Kashmiri Islam are remarkably unique.

Tourism has been devastated. The inaccessibility of the Kashmir Valley, and rumours of its beautiful gardens and lakes have long been a part of its mystique. Kashmir is still remarkably beautiful, but its vistas are now marred by sandbags and barbed wire. Few Indians or Pakistanis have seen the tragedy of Kashmir for themselves.

*   *   *   *   *

Days before I visited Kashmir in 2003, two militants tried to kill the Chief Minister, who at the time was Mufti Mohammed Sayeed. They fired rocket propelled grenades at his residence, killed two Border Security Force soldiers and then raced into the Ali Jan Shopping Complex across the street. Mohammed Altaf, owner of the Al Karam Interior Decoration Collection, whose shop is at the entrance to the complex, saw the armed men run by him – they were 10 feet away. As they raced into the building, he ran out, leaving his shop abandoned and unlocked. The resulting day-long carnage paralysed business and badly damaged the shopping complex: "Pakistan blames India and India blames Pakistan," Altaf told me. "In the middle, Kashmir gets destroyed."

The building is a relatively open structure, with a central staircase opening onto shops – but the heavily armed militants kept Indian troops at bay for a whole day and night. One used a landing as a bunker. The structure of the stairs provided a small triangular opening from which to shoot at soldiers climbing the stairs. Another used a room in the rear of the building, which also provided natural cover. The walls and stairs of the shopping complex were riddled with hundreds of bullet holes when I visited; the stairs were chipped and brick walls had been exposed by grenade explosions. Bloodstains were visible on the landing where the first militant was killed; the room in the rear was too badly damaged to retain evidence of human occupation. The outcome of the attack was certain death for the militants, their motivation was apparently to win publicity for the cause of Kashmiri separatism. "They came here for death, to die here," said one shopkeeper, who identified himself only as Ahmed. "One thing I will say," he said of the militants in a tone of admiration. "Whatever weapons they had, they used." Ahmed estimated that it had taken three thousand security troops to kill the militants after the two men had run out of ammunition and grenades. Ahmed said some 80 soldiers had been injured. And the militants were calm throughout the siege: During the overnight barrage of gunfire, Ahmed said, they had brewed themselves tea.

As Ahmed finished his account, nearly two dozen heavily armed Indian soldiers poured out of three jeeps in the parking yard below. They took up positions along the front of the complex, and others fanned out in pairs to the other floors. Two arrived in the area where I was conducting my interview; they watched me carefully but asked no questions. There was the crackle of walkie-talkie conversation. I cautiously climbed down the steps. Two soldiers armed with automatic rifles stood inside the Al Karam Interior Decoration Collection. Two officers with walkie talkies stood beside them, monitoring reports from other floors. A man in civilian clothes was fingering pieces of fabric. His name was Raj Bonsi, and he was shopping for curtains. All the soldiers in the complex were there to protect him. Mohammed Altaf gave Bonsi two swatches of cloth with the prices written on them. Bonsi cordially shook hands with me, told me his name but declined to give his rank. "The only thing we are afraid of is journalists," he said, laughed and waved goodbye. Holding his swatches, he disappeared into the middle jeep. The heavily armed soldiers backed away from the shopping complex, their fingers on triggers, and the vehicles pulled away.

* * * * *

"Don't import ideas for which the society is not ready," said the top official of the Border Security Force in Kashmir. The Indian paramilitary outfit was responsible at the time for counter-insurgency operations, especially in cities like Srinagar. A group of journalists had asked Vijay Raman, the Inspector General of the BSF, about human rights violations by Indian security forces in Kashmir.

I happened to visit Kashmir during the month of Ramadan, where Muslims break daylong fasts at an evening meal called the *iftar*. The term has coined a new phrase – *iftar* diplomacy. Various groups in Kashmir organise meals after sundown, using the occasion to break bread – and break the ice – with friends and adversaries. Raman, a Hindu, had invited local journalists to an *iftar* dinner. A half dozen reporters were clustered around him on the lawn of the BSF headquarters in Srinagar when I arrived, and one of them had asked him about human rights. Top officials of the force hovered nearby, and cuisines from all across India were being prepared under a series of tents on one side of the lawn. It was approaching sundown.

I asked Raman what he meant when he said that India was not ready for ideas about human rights. The other journalists melted away – I imagined they had heard him talk about this before. Raman invited me back into his office since it was getting chilly. He wore military fatigues and his shirt sleeves were rolled into a smart cuff above his elbows. He sat behind his desk and lit a cigarette.

"You want to change society, but it has to have its own pace," he said. "The moment you accelerate it, you will upset the equilibrium. Particularly in Jammu and Kashmir, they have felt exploited. Even now they feel exploited. First by the Mughals, then by the Sikhs, then the British and now us. How can we redress this? We have interfered too much with social dynamics."

I asked him how this related to human rights concerns by groups in Kashmir, which have castigated both militants and security forces for widespread abuses; a group called the Association of Parents of Disappeared Persons issued a public statement while I was in Kashmir saying that 104 people like Haider Ahmed Bhat had vanished during the previous year alone.

"Spare the rod and spoil the child," Raman replied. "If you see Indian society, an elder's frown used to be bad enough. Now you are questioning the right of the elder to castigate. Our society is still developing. To impose these restrictions ..." He trailed off.

I asked him whether he was concerned that the sweeps and cordoned searches would alienate civilians. Raman said the sweeps were justified because the militants could not elude security forces without support from local Kashmiris. He pulled out his wallet and produced a one thousand rupee note. It looked genuine, but he showed a series of small discrepancies that proved it was counterfeit: "Made in a Pakistan mint," he said. "We find this among the local population. A person comes to a rural area, spends time. The expenditure may be five hundred rupees, but they give this note. It's worse than an AK-47."

I pressed him again on how this related to human rights violations. Raman leaned forward, and pointed to his uniform.

"Several innocent people have been killed by this khaki uniform," he said, a startling admission from a senior Indian security official. But Kashmiris were not inherently opposed to ruthless tactics, Raman said: "You kill a real militant in cold blood in (downtown) Lal Chowk, there will be celebrations in Srinagar. People here have not seen trains, not seen the sea, not seen theatres. It is these people who want a change." A short while later, Raman's aides summoned him into the lawn for dinner. Before I left, I was introduced to a young officer called

Pramod Kumar who had been injured in the recent shopping complex siege. Kumar had been hit in the left hand by a bullet and received splinters on the right side of his torso.

*   *   *   *   *

Everyone in Kashmir has some direct link to the trauma of the last 15 years. Muzaffar Ahmed, the director of health services for the state, said virtually every home had seen relatives, friends or neighbours killed, maimed or abducted. Psychiatrists in Srinagar used to see 50 cases a day before the troubles began, they now see more than 350. Many of the problems are related to stress—corrosive fear has become omnipresent. The doctors are often as frightened as patients: One of Ahmed's ambulance drivers was killed a few weeks before my visit in northern Baramullah District by unknown gunmen, another had a leg blown off and now drives with a prosthetic limb. A third ambulance driver was killed in army crossfire in 1996. Many Kashmiris told me that the conflict has spiralled beyond control, with ordinary citizens terrified by militants into offering harbour, and then terrified by the security forces for cooperating with the militants. Each successive round of escalation is met with reprisal, each reprisal with escalation.

"If India says Pakistan is supporting militants, then India is supporting army militants, too," said Zahoor Shah, a lawyer in Srinagar, whom I interviewed shortly after Friday prayers at the city's historic Hazratbal Mosque, a shrine said to contain a hair of the prophet Mohammed. Shah said there were stacks of files in Srinagar's high court describing the cases of missing people.

The carnage is all the more tragic because for decades, Kashmir was one of the few places in South Asia where Hindus and Muslims lived in genuine harmony. When India was partitioned in 1947, Hindus and Muslims slaughtered one another across several states, but Kashmir remained largely peaceful. Family names – potent signals of caste, creed and family origin – are shared between Hindus and Muslims in Kashmir; names like Pandit and Bhat are commonly used by both communities. A tradition of Sufism ran through the region, where saints fused different religions into songs of universal divinity. All that has now changed. Hundreds of Kashmiri Hindus were killed in the late 1980s in a systematic campaign of terror; thousands of their relatives fled, abandoning homes and history, to live in refugee camps to the south. Militant groups in Kashmir now threaten women who wear western attire, and force Kashmiri men to adopt rigid Islamic codes. In turn, Indian nationalists have insisted that force be met with force in Kashmir. Security troops in Kashmir, who are drawn from all over India, are predominantly Hindu, adding to the sense that the army is an occupying force, and the conflict is based on a religious divide. Most Indians dismiss the notion that the hundreds of thousands of soldiers in Kashmir represent an occupation; the air force officer I spoke with asked me, "how can anyone call it an occupation when Kashmir is a part of India? It is merely a domestic disturbance." But the presence of armed soldiers on virtually every street certainly has the feel of an occupation. Militants in Kashmir are hidden among the population, and fighting them necessarily involves civilian casualties – and resentment. "Whether it is militants or security forces, we are suffering. As citizens we are suffering. The army hurts us more than the militants," said Hafsa Hafeez, a graduate student I interviewed at the University of Kashmir campus in Srinagar. Her father's cousin was killed after trouble broke out at a funeral procession and security forces opened fire. Another student, Arshad Khaleel, said he expected the security forces would never leave his homeland. Kashmiris routinely refer to what "Indians and Pakistanis" are doing – whatever New Delhi and Islamabad may say, many Kashmiris already feel they are a distinct people.

The Kashmir conflict regularly threatens the larger security of South Asia: In December 2001, armed militants seeking Kashmiri separatism stormed the entrance to the Indian parliament in Delhi; guards killed them just before they could lob grenades onto hundreds of national lawmakers. An influential section of India's intelligentsia believes the Kashmir dispute will be conclusively settled only through a fourth and final war with Pakistan. Officials in Islamabad have warned such talk could provoke nuclear war. Some Indians actually discuss how many cities they can afford to lose before Pakistan is obliterated. During a previous reporting assignment, one nationalist politician told me, "before the pride and sovereignty of my country ... nuclear war is a small thing."

There is a widespread sense in Kashmir that the conflict is endless. Nightlife is non-existent even in a big city like Srinagar; by sundown the streets are deserted. Health director Ahmed and his wife Shamim Naik, who is also a doctor, said families virtually never eat dinner at restaurants; friends do not meet for social occasions after sundown; there are no movie theatres. We had met for dinner at a restaurant attached to my hotel. It was 8:20 pm and we were the only patrons. The restaurant was dimly lit, and a mirror along one wall reflected the gloomy room. Ahmed told me that on his drive home, his car would be stopped seven times – he recited the precise location of each checkpoint. At every stop, he would have to show identification and be searched. As he drove, he would have to keep the light on inside the car, so that security forces hidden in bunkers would know they were dealing with a civilian. Ahmed grew angry as he described the daily indignities of life in Kashmir. Abruptly, Shamim Naik shushed her husband. Two men had entered the restaurant and were sitting in the far corner of the room. Ahmed froze in mid-sentence and switched the conversation to inconsequential chit-chat. In the mirror, I saw reflections of the men, and thought it odd they never took their eyes off us. After several minutes, a waiter brought the men a take-out order and they left. But the conversation at our table was over. Kashmiris do not know when they are being overheard, or by whom. Ordinary people do not know whom to trust. Many people declined interviews – one professor at the University of Kashmir examined my business card, which identified me as a reporter, shrugged and said, "how do I know who you are?" Militants wear the uniforms of security forces, security forces wear civilian clothes. An alphabet soup of intelligence agencies from India and Pakistan maintain different networks of informers. Someone at the table quoted a proverb about what happens to ordinary people when fear becomes commonplace: "If you tell me it's day, I'll say it's day. If you tell me it's night, it's night."

* * * * *

When I returned to my room on the third floor after dinner, the room was icy cold. There was no central heat in the hotel although temperatures in Srinagar touch freezing in November, and the space heater in my room was malfunctioning. I donned gloves and an extra pair of socks in preparation for a night patrol with the Border Security Force – one of Vijay Raman's men had promised to pick me up around

10 to show me how security forces monitored Kashmir at night. The soldiers arrived at 10:15, and I got a panicky call from the reception desk, which thinks of sundown as the end of business. A half dozen armed soldiers were in the lobby. I confirmed I was on my way downstairs. "You're coming down?" the clerk asked incredulously. The deputy commander of BSF Battalion 118, Sandeep Sinha, sat on a sofa in the lobby. He was about my height, but stockier. We shook hands. I dropped off my room key with the reception desk. "You're going with them?" the clerk asked, even more incredulous. I stepped outside with the soldiers. The temperature was not far above freezing. Two jeeps were stationed outside. Sinha walked ahead and one of the other soldiers came up suddenly. "One minute," he said, and ran a gloved hand under my arms, and inside my jacket. He squeezed my camera pouch. The soldiers formed a loose circle around me as I was searched. Then they asked me to get into the passenger seat of one jeep and Sinha took the wheel. The second jeep swung behind us. Half a mile on, we slowed at a roadblock, a metal bar across the road operated by a pulley system. Sinha stopped about 40 feet from the barrier, and doused his headlights. One of the soldiers jumped out of the back of the jeep and identified himself. The gate was raised and we drove through. Half a mile later, we repeated the process at a second checkpoint. The streets were deserted, the houses shuttered. No lights came from any windows. Srinagar could have been a ghost city. As we drove past the third roadblock, I asked Sinha why there were no people on the streets. "The people are there," he replied. "They are all in bunkers." The security forces were indeed everywhere, hidden behind sandbag fortifications, in pillboxes whose openings were draped with gunny sacks, a variety of barrels poking through. After a few moments, Sinha realised my question was about civilians, not

soldiers. "The civilians go to sleep early," Sinha said, explaining that it was Ramadan, and the people of Srinagar "have to wake up early" to eat before dawn. We drove on. We passed two more checkpoints, one of which trained a brilliant spotlight on us for several moments. Finally, we pulled up at the battalion headquarters. This time, the soldier who jumped out from the jeep raised his arms as he walked toward the elevated sentry booth. After he identified himself, he and other soldiers removed a series of obstacles – a set of metal poles inserted into holes in the ground, a metal plate with spikes pointing in both directions and a waist-high roll of barbed wire placed on either side of the gate. Sinha drove through and stopped the jeep in a dark courtyard, as the soldiers re-erected the barricades. I stepped out. Heavily armed soldiers watched me carefully. I made sure I didn't make any sudden movements. Sinha ushered me into a building and we entered a living room ringed with sofas. There was a five foot-long framed picture of the New York City skyline on the wall. Sinha explained that the house belonged to the owner of a flour mill; the soldiers had taken over both the mill and the owner's house after the business went bankrupt. He referred to the flour mill owner as "the landlord." The picture belonged to the landlord, Sinha said, and the soldiers had left it hanging in deference to his wishes. Sinha excused himself, and returned wearing a bullet-proof vest. He called for an assistant and asked for cigarettes. He told me he had a degree in economics; the commanding officers had college degrees while the enlisted men had 10th grade educations. As he smoked, Sinha proudly told me that he was from Jharkhand, "the newest state in India." Jharkhand was carved from the northern state of Bihar after a lengthy campaign for 'liberation.' Struggles for statehood and secession are underway elsewhere – numerous conflicts over ethnicity, language and religion have created a volatile stew of separatist struggles in both India and Pakistan – Jharkhand was one of three new Indian states formed in 2000. Sinha seemed unaware of the irony of soldiers like himself suppressing similar, if more radical, aspirations in Kashmir.

We stepped outside the landlord's house. About two to three dozen soldiers were milling in the dark. I was the only one not wearing any protective gear. Sinha instructed me to stay by his side and we set off, entering the street through a narrow opening. A black dog curled up outside the battalion headquarters jumped up and fell into step beside us – the stray marched with the soldiers on their night patrols. Sinha and the others all carried carbines, rifles and other weapons. We walked along a lane for about half a mile before entering the village of Machua. The moon was nearly full and the soft light on the houses and buildings accentuated the darkness of windows, and the shadows of houses under construction. Sinha drew me against a wall and instructed his men to search a partially constructed building, to make sure militants were not using it as a hideout. He mentioned that soldiers had apprehended a militant here two years ago. The soldiers fanned out, some took defensive positions while others shone flashlights into dark corners of the building. Finally, the men gave a signal and we pressed on. I did not see any villagers, but dogs greeted us with cacophonous barking. Our approach must have obvious to any militant hiding within a mile. Sinha turned sharply into a field, which was divided into plots by narrow ridges. Walking on the eight inch-ridges was difficult in the moonlight, and I stepped into the plots from time to time. The ground was loamy. The barking was left behind. "Dogs spoil our surprise," Sinha told me. "That's why we use the fields for special operations." I looked behind me; dozens of armed soldiers were fanned out in the moonlight. After a quarter mile we reached a clump of woods and Sinha cut through them to reach the bank of the river Doodhganga. The terrain was unpredictably hilly, the ground slushy and Sinha regularly left the edge of the river and took his men through wooded sections. At one point, as we passed a grove to our left, Sinha instructed one soldier to come up beside me, and warned him to keep a sharp eye on the grove because I was not wearing a bullet-proof vest. A chiaroscuro of moonlight and shadows surrounded us. The hike would have been strenuous in broad daylight, but given the darkness, it demanded complete concentration. We followed the river for half a mile, before cutting across to the village of Karalpura, where Sinha led us to a bridge. It was a well-known crossing point for militants, he said. Some of the soldiers crouched at one end and looked across the bridge through night vision goggles, others crossed the span and checked the underside. We had walked two and a half miles from the battalion headquarters; throughout the night, patrols like this fanned out across different routes every three hours or so. Sometimes, Sinha said his men stationed themselves at a location to monitor an area for several hours. The walk back was easier, since Sinha took us through village streets. We talked as we walked; Sinha told me he was 36 and that he didn't spend time thinking about the political situation in Kashmir. I asked him how many militants there were in the valley. Fewer than 2,000, he said. But that didn't include tacit support from a large part of the civilian population, he added, and this support made the militancy difficult to stamp out. I asked him if he had got used to the danger, and he replied that his family in Jharkhand asked him the same thing all the time. He said he had been in Kashmir and other trouble spots for a decade and no longer thought about the danger. But there was no doubt it was a dangerous, difficult life. Soldiers in Sinha's unit, often drawn from poor villages across India, visited their families and children for only a few weeks each year. They were in an alien land, unable to speak the local Kashmiri language, fighting shadows hidden among a resentful people. Constantly under threat, it was only natural that they would begin to view the entire populace with suspicion – trust would inevitably be exploited. Sinha was the last of several military officials to tell me there was no military solution to the insurgency.

We returned to the battalion headquarters at 1:15 am. Sinha and half a dozen soldiers drove me back to my hotel. There were fewer checkpoints; the streets were still deserted. And then, in the distance, we saw a lone man shuffling along the other side of the road. Sinha swerved the jeep across the road, braked and rolled down his window beside the man, who looked like he was in his seventies.

"Who are you?" Sinha asked brusquely in Hindi.

The man wore loose clothes, and he was carrying a bag under a shawl.

"Nothing sir, nothing sir–" The man had his arms raised already.

A soldier leaped out of the back of the jeep. He approached the old man at considerable velocity, one hand on his trigger. The soldier performed a rough search. "What are you doing here?" the soldier barked. The old man, now clearly terrified, kept repeating, "nothing sir, nothing sir."

Sinha instructed the soldier to let the man go. The soldier

climbed back into the jeep, which pulled away. There were no explanations provided for the search, no courtesies exchanged. India had probably lost another Kashmiri heart.

*   *   *   *   *

The two and a half hour drive to Sopore was lined with roadside messages exhorting people to forget about the troubles in the Kashmir valley, to ignore the heavy army presence in the countryside, and to think of the state as a halcyon tourist destination. "It is not the Rally, Enjoy the Valley" one said. "Our job is to make the whole world see the beauty of Kashmir," read another. I passed security facilities on the way out of Srinagar, pillboxes laced with camouflage netting, tall walls and taller observation posts. Guns pointed in all directions. There was little reduction in military presence as I left the city; soldiers patrolled in front of shops, there were checkpoints at bridges, armed troops stood on village rooftops. I took a photograph of the passing countryside; when I zoomed in on the digital image, I found a camouflaged soldier in the woods. Many soldiers wore masks that covered their noses and mouths; a local journalist I was travelling with said it was to avoid being identified. Convoys of military trucks rumbled past – one took 20 minutes and must have included some 200 vehicles. Gunners stuck out from the tops of vehicles; others had soldiers in the rear, weapons ready.

According to local newspapers, the residents of Sopore had held a march the previous evening to protest the killing of Haider Ahmed Bhat. The protest was led by Syed Ali Shah Geelani, one of the more radical Kashmiri separatist leaders. It is not clear how much support various leaders have among Kashmiris since they are self-appointed. State elections conducted in Kashmir in 2002 were supposed to hear the voice of the people, but turnout was very low in troubled areas: threats by militant groups, boycotts by separatist leaders and extraordinary security measures suppressed voting in the places where representative government is most desperately needed. While turnout in the state was fifty-five per cent overall, it was led by Hindu-majority Jammu. Local journalists told me that voter turnout in the Kashmir valley stood at twenty-two per cent, and was less than ten per cent in places like Srinagar. "The state government has no legitimacy," said Zahoor Shah, the Srinagar high court lawyer I interviewed. "If I was the Election Commissioner, I would have declared the election invalid." Low turnout was also reported in national parliamentary elections in 2004 after militants ordered a boycott. Geelani has not participated in the Hurriyat Conference talks with New Delhi.

We arrived at Sopore at noon. It was a dusty, chaotic town with a maze of winding streets, mud paths and open-air markets. Hawkers sold clothes from pavement heaps; people crowded around shacks that brewed endless cups of tea. Soldiers inspected passing vehicles. An old man sat in an empty field, his back to a tree. A few paces away, a soldier stood with a black mask over his nose and mouth. Crowds huddled around open fires. Most people wore the brown ankle-length gowns called pherans, many also carried baskets of live coals called kangadis which are used as portable heaters. It was drizzling. My driver asked for directions and we were directed to the neighbouring village of Gonipura. We pulled onto a mud path and bounced over uneven terrain. My head hit the roof of the van. A bridge took us over the Pohair River and then we were in Gonipura. We were surrounded by men before we had come to a stop. Their expressions were suspicious. Two led me into a courtyard ringed by several houses. Under a tent on one side, about three dozen women sat on the ground. Many veiled their faces as I approached. News of a journalist's arrival spread, and soon a crowd of more than a hundred men surrounded me. They drew me inside a nearby house. I sat cross-legged on the bare floor. The room had blue walls and wooden rafters. Men streamed in, all wearing pheran gowns. Some carried kangadis. The room was no more than 10 feet by 12 feet in size, yet 40 or 50 people crowded inside, and others peered in from the door and through the windows. Mohammed Ashraf, a man with sharp angular features and a neighbour of the Bhat family, and Ghulam Rasool Bhat, the dead man's uncle and an eye-witness to the abduction, narrated what had happened. The village had been searched repeatedly in the days leading up to October 21, they said, by soldiers from an Indian paramilitary unit called the 24 Rashtriya Rifles. Security forces searching for militants had stormed houses and interrogated villagers. This was considered routine, which was why the villagers had not thought it unusual when a white sport utility vehicle pulled up at Haider Ahmed Bhat's shop. The young man had just returned from Sopore with bread, which he had planned to sell. "He was picked up in the presence of the army," said Ghulam Rasool Bhat, who saw two men inside the vehicle in army uniforms. As Bhat gave cigarettes to one of the men who approached him, another grabbed him. Ashraf seized the dead man's uncle by the back of his neck to demonstrate how his neighbour had been captured; he pressed down on the uncle's head to show how the men had shoved Haider Ahmed Bhat into the vehicle. Relatives immediately lodged a complaint with the police. They also approached the army. No information was forthcoming. But army searches of the village abruptly ended, confirming villagers' suspicions that security forces had found what they were looking for. Three weeks later, word came from the Kangan police station, an outpost 75 miles away. Army officials had handed over Bhat's body to the Kangan police, who summoned Bhat's relatives. Where Haider Ahmed Bhat had left his village shoeless, he now wore boots. He had been wearing blue clothes; the corpse wore white. Ashraf touched his head behind his left ear, his chest and right shoulder to indicate where the villagers had found bullet wounds. "We don't know if it is a custodial killing or an encounter," Ashraf told me in English. "It could have been a custodial killing and then they took the body and made it a fake encounter." The villagers said they had no redress: disappearances, abductions and killings were too commonplace. The license plate on the sport utility vehicle that picked up Haider Ahmed Bhat was determined to be fake – no such number was registered with the state. Ghulam Rasool Bhat told me it was the third such abduction in Gonipura. "What can we do against the security forces?" he asked. "We are helpless." The family brought the corpse back to Gonipura for the funeral. The dead man was survived by his parents, three brothers and four sisters. I could hear a steady wailing from the tent with the mourning women. I asked if I could speak with Haider Ahmed Bhat's parents. The mother was too distraught, I was told, but the father might be willing to talk to me. I asked the uncle about the political arguments between India and Pakistan over Kashmir. He waved his hand. "We first require our safety," he replied.

The dead man's father entered the room. Mohammed Ahsan Bhat was 62, and he began to weep before he sat down on the ground. For several moments, the room was silent. I could ask him no questions, for he simply held his cheeks and rocked and tears flowed along the wrinkles on his face. The others consoled him. "He was a nice boy, very obedient," he said finally in Kashmiri, and the local journalist I was with translated the words. "He had no links with any militants. We don't know why he was picked up." The father relapsed into tears. "We can only cry," the uncle said finally. "We pray to Allah for our safety. What else can we do?"

The villagers escorted me back into the courtyard. They had bitter words for the state government, which had promised "a healing touch." Some called it "a killing touch." Women beat their chests as I took photographs; the dead man's sister, Kulsuma Akhtar, sang her grief as she described how her brother had been abducted. Men walked beside my van as we pulled out of the village. Through the windows, they repeated details of the story over and over, like people who are afraid they will never be heard.